PENGUIN ESSENTIALS

ARE YOU EXPERIENCED?

William Sutcliffe is the author of ten novels, including the international bestseller *Are You Experienced?* and *The Wall*, which was shortlisted for the 2014 CILIP Carnegie Medal. His work has been translated into twenty-six languages. He lives in Edinburgh.

Drew Millward is a former child, artist, illustrator and adult. He was born in Coventry in 1981. Shortly after that, he moved to Bolton, Greater Manchester, where he grew up. It was uneventful. Drew went on to study Fine Art at Leeds Metropolitan University, during which time he became involved in the music scenes there, while neglecting his studies. His start in the world of graphic art came in the form of making posters for the shows he, and some friends, promoted. Thirteen years later he has worked for a vast, international client base and is still learning how to do things. He lives in a quarry, on a hill, in Yorkshire, with his wife.

Drewmillward.com

Are You Experienced?

WILLIAM SUTCLIFFE

PENGUIN BOOKS

PENGUIN ESSENTIALS

UK | USA | Canada | Ireland | Australia
India | New Zealand | South Africa

Penguin Books is part of the Penguin Random House group of companies
whose addresses can be found at global.penguinrandomhouse.com.

Penguin
Random House
UK

First published by Hamish Hamilton 1997
Published in Penguin Books 1998
This Penguin Essentials edition published 2017
001

Printed in Great Britain by Clays Ltd, St Ives plc

A CIP catalogue record for this book is available from the British Library

ISBN: 978-0-241-98120-7

www.greenpenguin.co.uk

MIX
Paper from
responsible sources
FSC® C018179

Penguin Random House is committed to a
sustainable future for our business, our readers
and our planet. This book is made from Forest
Stewardship Council® certified paper.

For Georgie

Zeus who leads mortals on the road to understanding,
Zeus who has ordained that wisdom comes through suffering.

Aeschylus – *Agamemnon*

It feels much better than it ever did, much more sensitive.

John Wayne Bobbitt

PART ONE

Bad planning

She's acting differently

'This seat doesn't go back properly.'

'Of course it does.'

'It doesn't.'

'Look. Let me show you.' I wrestle with the aeroplane seat. It won't budge. 'You're right. It's broken.'

She smirks – in a half-hidden way, which is the most hostile way she could do it. She's hiding it as if to say, 'You're a jerk who can't take the fact that I'm laughing at you.' A few weeks ago, she would have grabbed me by the ears, laughed in my face and called me an impotent chauvinist twat. Now she shows me just enough of a smirk to let me know that she's noticed me being an idiot, but that I'm not allowed to share it with her.

'Can we change seats?'

I don't answer. I arrived at the airport on time, checked in (asking specifically for a window-seat), and waited an hour and a half for Liz, who turned up with minutes to spare, *and* didn't even have any traveller's cheques on her and had to get the whole lot at the airport and there was only one place open and if that had been closed I don't know what we would have done. I'd . . . I'd have been travelling to India alone for three months. Or I'd have had to lend her my money for God's sake – but we would have run out half-way through – it wouldn't have been possible – and it's not my job to lend her money. I wouldn't have done it. She had weeks to get herself organized . . .

'Can we change seats? You're reading anyway – you don't need to lean back. I want to sleep.'

She's lying. We've only just taken off, and it's a clear day. There are still excellent views. I specifically wanted a window-seat so that I could see the views – and I know it's childish, but I love flying, O K ? I'm not ashamed of the fact that I enjoy the view from an aeroplane. So maybe I am a bit old for that, but I don't care. I just happen to be interested in it.

'David . . . ? Are you *lis*tening?'

She glares at me, her features arranged into a look of absolute scorn which says 'I dare you to tell me that you just want to see the view. I *dare* you. Go on, say it. Then it'll be out in the open – we won't be able to deny – either of us – that you are a twelve-year-old in the body of a nineteen-year-old – that you have no shame about being an absolute prick.'

I'm not being paranoid – it's all there, written into the curve of her nostrils and the squint.

The most annoying thing is that I wasn't really reading. I was only glancing at my book, and was really looking out of the window. But now she's caught me in the act I can't tell her that I wasn't really reading, because that's exactly what she wants me to say to make me look selfish.

'All right,' I say. 'In a few minutes.'

I close the book and pointedly look out of the window to demonstrate that I'm not selfish, and that switching seats is a significant sacrifice. I hear Liz sigh, and out of the corner of my eye, I can see her shaking her head. She's fixed it so that whatever I do, it confirms what she thinks of me.

She hates me. She thinks I'm immature, selfish, bigoted

and arrogant. I'm giving her my seat, for God's sake – at some point, *I'm* going to want to sleep, and I won't be able to because I've given *her* the reclining seat – and she's sitting there shaking her head because *I'm* selfish. It's outrageous.

I don't understand why it's happened. I don't know what's changed. A few weeks ago, we were best friends – we were almost in love. Now we're stuck together, heading to India for three months, and she's treating me like a piece of rotten meat. Maybe I *am* immature, selfish, bigoted and arrogant, but she used to like me. I haven't changed. So I don't see why I should alter my behaviour now, just because she's acting differently.

Pure blind fear

I had heard the old cliché about how when you arrive in India, it's like stepping into an oven, but this hadn't prepared me for the fact that when you arrive in India, it *is* like stepping into an oven.

Delhi airport was ... it was just taking the piss. That number of people simply couldn't fit into such a small space and not end up eating each other. It wasn't possible. And no one else even seemed to notice that it was crowded.

After queuing for several hours at immigration, we escaped the airport and discovered that it was even madder outside. The minute we were in the open air, several rugby teams of smelly men launched themselves at us and tried to pull us to bits, so that we could send separate limbs to town on different forms of transport. It was disgusting. I felt like I was being mugged. Mugged while inside an oven. And all the guys who were trying to get us into their taxis looked so poor and desperate that I just wanted to go home straight away.

Liz noticed that the other backpackers from our flight had got on a bus, so we breast-stroked through the crowd and clambered in behind them. The engine was already on, and we took our seats, relieved that we had made it in time. The driver pointed angrily at our bags, then at the roof of the bus. I noticed that no one else on the bus had their bags with them, so we got out of the bus and found ourselves back in a different crowd of people, all of whom seemed to be offering to put our stuff on the roof of the bus. I was convinced that they'd steal our rucksacks the minute I turned my back so I tried to climb up myself, but some guy with a red turban on, which gave him the appearance of being the chief bag-putter-on-roofer, pulled me off the ladder and tugged at my bag. I relented, and let him take our rucksacks. I watched him all the way and saw him lash down the bag with a rope. He looked as if he knew what he was doing, and there were several other bags up there already, so I decided that maybe it was all reasonably legal. When he came back down, he started doing a strange upward nodding gesture and saying 'munee – munee'.

'He wants money,' said Liz.

'Why should I give him money? It's his job. I was quite willing to put it up there myself.'

'Just give him some money, for God's sake. I'll get in and grab some seats.'

'I haven't got any money yet, have I? It doesn't exactly look like he takes traveller's cheques.'

'Just give him anything.'

'Like what? A roll of loo paper? Yesterday's *Guardian*?' She ignored me and got on the bus.

'Munee. Munee.'

'I haven't got any.'

'Munee.'

He was beginning to tug at my clothes now, and the crowd of onlookers was closing in.

'Look, mate – I haven't got any money yet. I have to go to a bank.'

'MUNEE!'

I turned out my pockets to show him that I didn't have any money, and out fell a whole load of English coins. He gave me an evil stare, then bent over to pick up the coins. There was a mini riot while several people scrabbled for the cash, so I sneaked away and got into the bus, hoping that I'd be out of sight before they realized that it was only English money.

During the bag episode all the seats had gone, and Liz was standing somewhere near the back. I went and joined her.

'Just in time,' I said.

Half an hour later, with the bus jammed full of people, the driver started revving the engine.

Half an hour after that, with the bus containing twice as many people as it had when I'd thought it was full, and with the man in the red turban still shouting at me through the window, we crawled out of the airport.

'This is awful,' I said.

'What's awful?' said Liz.

'This. Everything.'

'What did you expect?' she said, with an unforgiving glare.

'Is this what it's meant to be like?'

'I suppose so.'

'This is what we've come for?'

'Yes. It's India.'

'Jesus. I don't believe this.'

I suddenly felt as if my stomach had been filled with pebbles. This was all wrong. I'd come to the wrong place. I hadn't even eaten anything yet, and I felt sick already – from the heat, the crowds, the claustrophobia – and pure blind fear.

What the hell had I done? Why had I come to this awful country? I was going to hate it. I already knew. There was no way I could possibly get used to any of this. And now I was stuck here.

This was bad. This was very bad.

J

After the bus dropped us off, we went to the Ringo Guest-House, which sounded cool, and was the first place mentioned in the Lonely Planet. It was a short walk from the bus-stop, down a side-street.

Not that our route bore much resemblance to what I'd call a street. There was no Tarmac for a start – just compacted mud which was thick with dust and dotted with green puddles, piles of rubbish and the odd cow-pat. Amazingly, most people were walking around in flip-flops.

I took a good look at the people, and they didn't look anything like the Indians in England. It wasn't that they looked *physically* different, or even that they were wearing weird clothes. There was something else I couldn't put my finger on that looked completely alien. Something in the way they moved, and in their facial expressions. Whatever it was, it scared the shit out of me. And wherever I looked there were hundreds of them – shouting at each other, or shouting at me to 'Take taxi', 'Eat best food' or 'Make international best rate telephone call' – all of them jostling past, laughing, chatting, arguing, and generally swaggering around as if they owned the place.

*

The hotel was up a dark staircase, and consisted of a few double rooms positioned off a cramped roof courtyard. A man with a fleshy golf ball growing out of the side of his neck told us that there were no double rooms available, so we'd have to take beds in the dorm. He then led the way up a ladder to a higher corner of the roof, on which a corrugated-iron hut had been built.

The metal walls and roof turned the dorm into even more of an oven than the rest of the country was anyway. The room was crammed with beds, and as my eyes adjusted from the outside glare to the murky dormitory, I could pick out a few depressed-looking travellers lying around on their beds. They all looked so thin and miserable that you could almost have mistaken the place for a prison. A few of them were reading, one was asleep, and a couple were simply lying on their beds staring into space.

This did not look like a bunch of people having fun. Having escaped the insanely frantic streets, we had somehow stumbled on something worse: a kind of morgue like gloom. Although we stood there for what must have been several minutes, no one so much as turned to look at us. Whatever was going to happen to me, I did not want to end up like those people. I wanted to go home.

Attempting to gauge how long I was stuck in India – to sense what three months really felt like, I suddenly felt dizzy with despair.

'What d'you reckon?' said Liz.

'Grim.'

'Mmm.'

'Do you think we'll get anywhere better?'

'Maybe.'

'We could always ask someone,' I said.

'The people here are bound to think this is the best place, or they wouldn't be here, would they?'

'I suppose so.'

The thought that this could be anyone's idea of the best place in Delhi was depressing beyond belief. Due to the heat, however, wandering around with our backpacks until we found somewhere we liked simply wasn't an option.

Liz fished the guidebook out of her pack, and we saw that there was one other recommended hotel in the area, called Mrs Colaço's. The book described it as 'basic, crowded and rather hard on the nerves,' which didn't sound particularly inviting, but it was the only one nearby that was mentioned, so we hauled ourselves through the hot, soupy air towards Mrs Colaço's.

This had a marginally less spirit-crushing atmosphere than Ringo's, and wasn't quite so full of catatonic hippies. Again, there were no actual rooms available, but we gratefully took dormitory beds, relieved to have at last found somewhere to flop.

We flopped.

Lying on my hard bed, staring at the ceiling fan, which was rotating just slowly enough to have absolutely no effect on the surrounding air whatsoever, I realized that I had never really *been* hot before. I mean, I'd had hot skin, in the sun, and I'd got hot from running around, but I'd never had this strange sensation of feeling like a slab of meat cooking from the inside. I genuinely felt full of heat – as if my limbs and internal organs were huge, half-cooked lumps that I had to carry around with me. And the breath coming out of my nose felt like a miniature hot-air dryer blowing on the skin of my top lip.

How could people live like this? How could a country function in these conditions? How could so much air possibly reach such a temperature without heating up the entire planet?

We couldn't unpack, since there was nowhere to put anything, so once we'd had a good flop, we didn't really know what to do. I had always wondered what travellers did all day – and now I was sitting on a bed in Delhi, having just arrived, not knowing what to do. We were both too hot and knackered to move, without the will or the courage to go outside and face the reality of being in India.

There was one other person in the room. He was lying on his back with his elbows on the bed and his hands in the air, staring into space. It looked like he was reading a book, except that his hands were empty.

'Hi,' said Liz.

'Peace,' he said.

'Peace,' she replied.

He sat up and gave her a lecherous look.

'What's your name?' said Liz.

'J.'

'J?' I said, in a tone of voice that somehow communicated the instant dislike I'd already taken to him – an impressive achievement, given that I only had one letter to play with.

'J – cool,' said Liz, trying to compensate for me.

'What's your real name?' I said.

'My real name?'

'Yeah.'

He had 'Public-School Git' stamped all over him.

'J.'

'That's what your parents call you?'

'No. It's short for Jeremy.'

'Right. Sorry, Jeremy. I mean, J.'

'Where are you from, J?' said Liz.

Jeremy chuckled, and gave her a long, meaningful look. She tried to avoid looking confused.

'You haven't . . . been here very long, have you?'

Liz forced out a bashful-young-virgin blush. 'No,' she said, fiddling with the bedsheet. 'We only just landed.'

'I could tell,' he said.

'Maybe it's the airline tags on our rucksacks?' I offered.

He ignored me. 'When you've been here . . . a few . . . months . . . you stop asking that question. You begin to belong as much to India as to your native land.'

'Right,' said Liz. 'I can imagine.'

'Where *are* you from, though?' I said.

He ignored me.

'England?' I said. 'We're English.'

Reluctantly, he nodded.

'Whereabouts?' I said.

'Oh . . . the south.'

'Excellent. So are we. London?'

'No.'

'Which town?'

He was pissed off now.

'Tunbridge Wells,' he said.

'Nice,' I said. 'Must freak you out being here. Coming from a rich area like that, I mean.'

'Not any more. Not any more,' he said, looking deep into Liz's eyes.

'How long have you been here?' she said.

He chuckled. 'Ohhh – long enough. Long enough to love it . . . and hate it. Long enough to wonder if I can ever go back.'

'What's that – a week?' I said.

Neither of them was amused.

'D'you get ill much, then?' I said.

'What do you mean by ill?'

He looked at me as if he'd said something devastatingly intelligent.

I looked at him as if he'd said something devastatingly stupid.

'You know – ill. Delhi belly. The shits.'

'Look – if you want to survive in this country – you've got to redefine your terms. Ill means one thing in the West and another thing in the East. An Indian accepts his fate – it's the West's constant fight against destiny that has created a nation of hypochondriacs. It's all so fleeting – to me it hardly matters.'

'I see you don't drink the water, though,' I said, nodding at the bottle of mineral water by his bed.

He scowled at me. Liz scowled at me.

'Do you mind if I have a sip, Jeremy – I mean, J?'

He nodded.

I realized I didn't want to share his germs, so I tried to drink without touching the mouth of the bottle, but it didn't really work, and most of it went down my front. I don't think they noticed, though.

Prompted by Liz, he started spouting off about all the places he'd been to, while she jotted down all his suggestions, muttering things like 'Wow, it sounds amazing!', 'I don't know if we're brave enough for that,' and 'Where exactly do you find the camel man . . . ?' After this had gone on for long enough to make me feel nauseous, I asked Liz to step into the corridor for a word.

'Why do we need to go outside?' she said, reluctantly looking up from Jeremy's maps.

'Because I want a word.'

'But . . .'

'In private.'

She exchanged looks with Jeremy, and stepped into the corridor with me. Before I had a chance to say anything, she laid into me.

'Why are you being so rude?'

'The guy's an arsehole.'

'There's no need to talk to him like that.'

'Why shouldn't I? He's a prick.'

'If you bothered to talk to him, you'd know that he's actually very nice.'

'Oh, come on . . .'

'He *is*. He's also been here a long time, and has a lot of information which both of us will find very useful.'

'And that's why you're flirting with him, is it?'

'I'm *not* flirting with him.'

'You are. He's been giving you the eye since the minute you walked in the room, and you're just lapping it up.'

'Oh, give me a break.'

'It's true. That's why I don't like him.'

'Oh, grow up.'

She spun round and returned to the dormitory.

I followed her in and said, 'Well you can stay here as long as you like – I'm going to take a look at the city.'

'Aren't you even interested in this?' she said. 'Don't you care where the good places are?'

'I'm absolutely fascinated, Liz. I really am. But there's a world out there to explore, you know. You can't hide from it much longer.'

I strode out, sensing victory, but feeling like a bit of a sad twat.

Outside, it was somehow even hotter than inside.

The hotel was in a quiet street, and I walked back towards the main road where the airport bus had dropped us off. Right, I thought. I'm walking down a street in India. I can handle this. I'm doing OK. Those look like proper houses, too – it's obviously not *such* a poor country.

Then some kid, who I have to admit did look pretty grubby, emerged from behind me and started tugging at my sleeve. She cupped her other hand in front of me.

That reminds me, I thought. I have to change some money.

'No, sorry,' I said, and started walking again.

The kid didn't let go of my arm, though. She just carried on walking down the street with me, tugging at my sleeve.

'No, sorry,' I said again.

She carried on tugging.

'Look – I haven't got any coins.'

She tugged harder, and whined a word at me that I couldn't understand.

'NO COINS,' I said, and walked off at a brisk pace.

Although she was now half running, she kept up with me and tapped my arm whenever she could reach it.

I stopped walking. 'LOOK – NO COINS. I'M GOING TO THE BANK NOW. NO MONEY.'

We stared at each other. She didn't flinch. It was clear that whatever I said, she wasn't going to leave me alone.

I set off again, as fast as I could without breaking into a run, but still she kept up with me. When I stopped, she tugged at my sleeve again.

'Get off,' I said.

She didn't move.

'Leave me alone.'

She stared at me, with enormous miserable eyes. I really did wish I had some money now, partly to get rid of her, but also because the sight of her made me feel like a disgusting human being. It felt as if she were an inhabitant of hell who had been sent to haunt me – to remind me how rich and lucky I was, and how I didn't deserve anything that I had.

I didn't *want* to be reminded how rich and lucky I was – especially since at that moment I was feeling particularly unlucky: trapped in unbelievable heat in a repulsive, filthy, threatening country, pinned to the spot by a five-year-old girl who wanted my money.

We stared at each other. I tried to stop myself thinking

about what kind of a life this girl must lead, and even fleetingly imagined that she was looking into my eyes, wondering what kind of life *I* led. A snapshot of home popped up in my mind, making me feel instantly homesick and guilty.

'Go away,' I said, weakly.

She didn't move. I took a couple of steps, and again she followed me, still tugging at my sleeve.

Exasperated, I turned round and pushed her away, gently enough for her not to fall over, hard enough to make her take a couple of steps backwards. She stayed there, still eyeballing me.

I walked away, and this time she didn't follow.

I tried not to let myself think about what had just happened. It was just something I would have to get used to. There must be a way of shrugging them off. There must be a way that Indians deal with it. I'd just have to learn.

For an instant, I felt excited. This was going to be a battle. I was at last properly challenging myself.

Then I felt depressed again. The pebbles were back in my stomach.

By now I was in the main street. Over the road, I could see a bank. I crossed over and went in.

They ignore it

When I got back to the hotel, Liz and Jeremy were curled up on a bed with a map of India, giggling together. As soon as I entered the room, they both stopped laughing and gave me guilty looks, followed by badly concealed smirks.

'Do either of you want to go and eat?' I said.

'Why not?' said Liz, giving me a weak don't-worry-nothing-happened smile.

'Where can you get a good Chinese round here?' I said.

They both frowned at me.

'Joke,' I explained.

'Oh, right,' said Jeremy. 'I see.'

'Where do you recommend?' said Liz, with a pout.

'A number of places,' said Jeremy. 'I presume you want vegetarian.'

'Of course.'

'What?' I said. 'You're not a vegetarian.'

'I am now,' said Liz. 'It's the best way to stay healthy. Eat what the locals eat. Indigenous food.'

'Did you tell her that?' I said.

'Of course. It's well known that the meat here is unhealthy. You only have to see the way it sits around covered in flies. Of course, I've been a vegetarian since I was five. I never could stomach the stuff, and it took me five years to get up the courage to say so. It's deeply ingrained in Western culture that the only *real* meal is a meat-based . . .'

'Are you saying that the meat here's not safe?'

'Absolutely.'

'You reckon that if I eat it I'll get sick.'

'Almost certainly, yes.'

'I don't believe this! Are you serious?'

'Of course I am.'

'No – you're joking, aren't you?'

'I'm not. It's common knowledge.'

'You are. You're joking.'

'Look – eat what you want. I couldn't give two shits. But I won't be around to carry you to hospital.'

The minute we stepped out of the hotel, the girl who had been trying to beg from me earlier started following us down the street, tugging each of our sleeves one by one. For a while, no one spoke.

Then, suddenly, Jeremy spun round, gave the girl a menacing look, and shouted in her face, 'NO. NO BAK-SHEESH.'

She didn't move.

'PSSHHT! PSSHHT!' He hissed at her, waving her away with his arms, trying to frighten her off as if she were an under-intelligent dog.

Then he grabbed her upper arm and shook her once, quite hard. Her expression remained totally blank, and she didn't move.

'PSSHHT!' he hissed.

This time she obeyed, quietly turning round, and heading back to her waiting spot outside the hotel.

The three of us walked on in embarrassed silence. I was shocked that Jeremy could be so callous. Registering the look on my face, he gave a you're-so-naïve-I'm-so-wise chuckle. 'They're not real beggars those children,' he said. 'They just target the tourist hotels. You'd never see an Indian giving them any money.'

'Looked like a beggar to me. She wasn't exactly plump, was she?'

'They're run by gang leaders who take whatever money they get.'

'The kids don't get anything?'

'Of course not. It's all run by pimps.'

'What happens if they end the day without any money, though?'

'Oh, I wouldn't worry about that,' he chuckled. 'They make a *lot* of money. Some soft-hearted soul who's just stepped off the plane will casually give them fifty rupees because they know sod all about the country. That's what one of those little children's fathers will earn in a week's honest labour. It's a terrible thing. Tourists who act like that completely screw up the local economy. And the kids are disgustingly persistent. It really shouldn't be allowed.'

This guy was a fascist. A hippie fascist.

'But you can't treat people like that,' I said.

Jeremy laughed again. 'It's the only way to survive. If you got upset by every beggar, you'd end up killing yourself. You have to lose your Western preconceptions about materialist wealth and deal with it in the same way as the Indians.'

'And how *do* Indians deal with it?'

'They ignore it.'

Jeremy was enjoying this. He thought it made him sound clever.

'Believe me,' he said, 'within a fortnight, you won't even notice the beggars any more.'

'How can you fail to notice someone when they're pulling on your sleeve and won't let go of you?'

'You just do. You get a look on your face – an impervious look which the beggars can spot, and they stop bothering you because they can tell that you've stopped noticing them and won't give them any money.'

'Why did that girl go after you, then?'

'She wasn't after me, she was after you two. I just did you a favour by getting rid of her. Besides, Delhi's different. They're more organized.'

'And you reckon,' said Liz, 'that within a fortnight they'll stop bothering us?'

'I guarantee it. They'll stop bothering you just as soon as you stop being scared of them.'

'We just have to toughen ourselves up a bit,' said Liz.

'Exactly. We're all far too pampered in the West. It's one of the best things about coming to India – you have to face up to horrible things and develop an immunity to them.'

'Who says immunity's a good thing?' I said.

'Look – if you don't develop it, you'll never be happy here,' said Jeremy with a sigh, suddenly bored with the conversation. 'It's as simple as that.'

'You're right,' said Liz. 'You're absolutely right.'

I saw the worry-line begin to move from her forehead, as she set her face into a new expression. Her chin jutted forward a fraction, and her eyes narrowed.

Liz had set about toughening herself up.

Here we go, I thought. As if she wasn't bossy enough already.

In the restaurant, only one part of the menu looked appetizing.

'Are you really serious about the meat thing? You're not just trying to convert me or something?'

'I'm not talking about it any more. Eat whatever you want, and enjoy it. I don't give a shit,' said Jeremy.

'I can't believe I've come all the way to India, and I can't even have a curry.'

'Of course you can have a curry,' said Liz. 'Just eat a vegetarian one.'

'That's not a bloody curry. That's a side dish.'

They ignored me.

'How did you find this place?' said Liz.

'Oh – I've been here lots of times. Just dug it out, I suppose. It's not in the book or anything.'

'Which book?' she said.

'The book. The Book. There's only one worth having.'

'We've got the Lonely Planet – is that the right one?' Her face was overcome with anxiety.

'It's not the right one.' He paused for effect. 'It's the only one.'

Liz sighed with relief.

'If it's not in The Book, how come there are so many Westerners here?' I said.

'Word of mouth.'

'And how come the whole menu's translated into English?'

Liz snapped. 'When are you going to stop sulking?'

'I'm not sulking.'

'If you don't like it, you shouldn't have come.'

'I *do* like it. I just need to get used to everything.'

'Well, stop whining all the time and make an effort.'

'I'm not whining.'

'You are whining. And you're being very hostile to Jeremy – I mean, to J.'

'No I'm not.'

'Yes you are.'

'J – am I being hostile towards you?'

23

'I think maybe you just feel a little threatened. It's perfectly natural.'

'Threatened? By *you*? Nauseated, maybe. Threatened – I'm afraid not.'

'Dave. Stop it. I'm not amused,' said Liz.

'What are you – my teacher or something?'

'Are you going to behave?'

'Liz – don't be . . .'

'Are you?'

'Jesus. OK, OK. I'm sorry. I'll *behave*.'

Liz gave me a hard stare, then clicked her fingers at the waiter.

'Waiter! We're ready to order.'

'No we're not!'

She glared at me.

'Was that a whine? Are you classing that as a whine?'

She glared harder.

'Fine. Sorry I spoke. I suppose I'll just have one of whatever you're having.'

'Very imaginative,' she said, and maliciously ordered something made of lentils.

It was a big moment taking my first mouthful of Indian food. I started with a few grains of rice. That seemed OK. It tasted of rice. I then moved on to the lentil dish, chewing slowly at first to see if anything strange was going to happen. It tasted hotter than most curries I had eaten, but went down easily enough and didn't seem to provoke any instant adverse reaction.

Due to my anxious state I didn't have much of an appetite, but I forced down most of my portion in the hope that it would help me keep my spirits up. For desert, we each had a malaria tablet.

*

On the way back from the restaurant, just before we arrived at the hotel, we were accosted by the same beggar. Having already failed with Jeremy and me, this time she targeted Liz.

The newly toughened Liz wasted no time, and after one tiny sleeve-tug, she spun round, grabbed the kid by the shoulder and said, 'NO – NO MONEY. GO HOME,' shaking her violently for emphasis. The girl, displaying considerably more skill than me at recognizing a psycho when she saw one, backed off immediately.

Liz marched on to the hotel, victory stamped on her jawline. I could read what was going on in her head. *Dave can't handle this*, she was thinking. *He's struggling. But me – I'm doing just fine. I can cope.*

For an instant, I felt the burnt-rubber aftertaste of a malaria tablet in the back of my throat. This whole thing just wasn't going to work.

It's not compulsory, you know

I had first met Liz only a few months previously. It was coming up to Christmas, and a group of us from school, all in the middle of our year off before university, were meeting up for a final drink together. The group was about to break up, with most of us setting off on various trips around the world.

James (nominally my best friend, but in fact we'd been getting on each other's nerves for at least three years) turned up with Paul, and with his new girlfriend – Liz. This struck me as slightly inappropriate. You don't really want a newcomer around when old friends are getting together for an emotional farewell. It's inhibiting.

'Have you two met?' he said, trying to sound casual. We both knew that he had told me all about her, in explicit and tedious detail, while deliberately keeping us apart. I had assumed that this meant he was embarrassed by Liz, and by her inability to live up to his ludicrous claims about her beauty, but one sight of her instantly demolished that theory. She was amazing. And exactly how he'd described her. With an affronted jolt, I realized that James hadn't introduced us because he was embarrassed by me.

'I don't *think* so,' I replied.

'Liz. Dave.'

'Hi,' she said, offering me a cheek to peck. (Fantastic skin, too.)

'And have I introduced you to these?' said James, taking a step back and indicating two pairs of identical brown-leather boots, sported by him and Paul.

'What the hell is that?' I said.

'Walking boots. Brand new,' replied James. 'We've done our final big shop. Look.' He lifted a huge green YHA-shop bag on to the table, and we all sat down.

'Rucksack; money belt; mosquito-repellent stick; mosquito-repellent spray; mosquito-repellent gel; water-purification tablets – eight packs; travel wash – four tubes . . .'

While the pile of junk mounted on the table, I caught sight of Liz's face. She was squinting slightly, and her mouth was set in an angry pout. James, you see, was doing his big trip with Paul (oldest friend and general obedient stooge), while Liz was stuck in London doing an art foundation course.

'. . . mini sewing kit; water-resistant torch; special sweat-absorbent socks; nylon emergency towel; rubber all-purpose sink plug; and, best of all . . . this.'

In his hand, James held out a palm-sized piece of square black plastic.

'What is it?'

'Da-daaah.' He prised open the plastic, revealing a square of paper which, after delicate unfolding, showed a map of the world.

The last thing I wanted to see was a map of the world, since it inevitably indicated that he was about to force-feed me with yet another account of the latest, infinitesimal changes to his 'master plan'. I opted for swift diversionary tactics.

'Walking boots? What do you need walking boots for?'

'For our trek. We're doing a trek in the . . .'

'Since when have you been into walking?'

'Since always.'

'Bollocks. You always said you hate the countryside. You think it's boring.'

'This is the Himalayas we're talking about, Dave. It's not *countryside*.'

'It is. It's just big countryside.'

'David – we're going to see three eight-thousand-metre peaks. Do you realize how many eight-thousand-metre peaks there are in the world?'

'No, and I'm not int–'

'Six.'

'Seven,' said Paul.

'It's six.'

'There are seven.'

'Six.'

I turned to Liz. 'Fascinating company, these two.'

She shrugged and half smiled at me.

'James,' I said, cutting in on their argument, 'you're boring. The pair of you are piss-boring. Talk to each other about your trip in private, OK? There are two other people here, and we'd like to stay awake, so can we try and talk about something real?'

'Hah,' said James.

'What do you mean, "hah"?'

'That's . . . just . . . not very elegant.'

'Elegant?'

'I mean – that kind of . . . open jealousy . . . is . . . is just embarrassing.'

'Oh, I *see*. I'm not bored – I'm jealous.'

'Yes.'

'And in my heart of hearts, I really am desperately inter-

28

ested in how many hills there are that are a little bigger than lots of other hills.'

'Dave – you can't face us talking about our trip because it reminds you that you are pissing away your year. You're pissing it away because you haven't planned anything, and you haven't planned anything because you're basically too scared to go travelling.'

'I'm going abroad.'

'To Switzerland?'

'Yes.'

'Oooh – aren't we brave? You're really risking life and limb there. Waiter in a Swiss hotel! Hazardous stuff.'

'Don't be an arsehole, James.'

'Shocking hygiene, too. You're going to get really ill in *Switzerland*.'

'James, you're being annoying,' said Liz. 'Maybe he wants to learn French. Or German. Which part of the country is it?'

'I'm going to the French-speaking bit, near to the . . .'

'Do you want to learn Fwench, David? Something pwac-tical for your CV?'

I could feel my face going red.

'You're jealous, and you're a coward,' he said. 'You can't face doing any real travel because you don't think you could survive in . . . in a different culture.'

'I could survive.'

'Why aren't you doing it, then?'

'Just . . .'

'Will you lay off him,' said Liz. 'Not everyone is like you, James. If he doesn't want to travel, he doesn't want to travel. It's not compulsory, you know.'

That was it. The moment I fell in love with her. Or started to fall in love with her.

James bit back a scowl and tried to smile. He didn't like

being contradicted in public by his girlfriend. (That's the kind of arsehole he was.) 'Yeah, but . . . I mean, you'd go travelling if you weren't stuck in your art foundation course.'

'I'm not *stuck* in an art foundation course. I chose to do an art foundation course.'

'Yeah, but if you had the time, you'd go off to Asia or something, wouldn't you?'

'I probably *will* go to "Asia or something". I've got a perfectly long summer holiday.'

'I know. We've discussed that. All I mean is, if you had a year off like Dave, you wouldn't waste your time pissing around in Europe.'

'And all *I* mean is, stop showing off. We all know where you're going. We think you're very clever and very brave. Now drop it.'

Silence descended. They stared at each other. Veins were standing out on James's temples. I was almost fainting with delight.

'Shall I get more drinks?' said Paul, with a cough. 'What do you . . . ? Um . . . how about the same again? . . . I'll get that, then.'

Paul retreated to the bar, his shoes squeaking slightly as he walked. James and Liz continued to stare at each other.

'I need the toilet,' I said, standing up. 'Oh, no I don't. I'll go later.' I sat down again, trying to hold in an evil smile. James gave me an angry look. I shrugged, pretending not to understand what he meant. Turning my head, I realized that Liz was also holding in a smile, but rather less effectively than me. A smirk was playing on her lips, and it wasn't directed at James, but at me.

'How long are you going to be in Switzerland, Dave?' she said.

'Just for the ski season. About four months.'

'Well, with Dr Livingstone here heading off, my social life is in danger of withering away. Will you give me a ring when you get back?'

Tunnel vision. Racing pulse. Cold sweat. 'Um . . . yeah. I haven't . . . um . . . got your . . .'

'Here's my number.' She pulled a pen from her bag, and wrote on a beer-mat.

'Thanks.' I smiled at her, and she blinked back. I turned to smile at James, but he seemed to be exhibiting the symptoms of advanced flu, and couldn't even look at me.

I know it's bad to think about your friends this way, but for several years it had been obvious to both of us that James had the better of me. It wasn't anything specific, but an accumulation of little things had put him on top. Now, with that beer-mat in my back pocket, for the first time since we were fifteen I felt as if I had the better of him.

I floated home from the pub, my fingers fluttering every few seconds to touch the small bulge, square with rounded corners, in the back of my jeans.

You are. You're asking me out

I had spent the first half of my year off working at the Sock Shop in King's Cross. When you work in a clothes shop, all you do is walk around folding up what the customers have unfolded. This makes the Sock Shop a particularly weird place to work, because you can't fold a sock. Your life begins to have so little meaning that you start wondering if you're still alive. After that, you even start doubting whether or not socks actually exist.

Most of my friends had done similar (though usually less surreal) jobs, and were now spending their money on a trip to India, South-East Asia or Australia. Everyone seemed to have big ideas about how they had to find themselves, whatever that meant, through some journey to a poverty-stricken flea-pit half-way up a malaria-infested mountain on the other side of the planet. There was a general belief that a long and unpleasant holiday was of crucial import-ance to one's development as a human being.

At this stage, I still had no plans for what I was going to do when I got back from Switzerland, but felt pretty certain that the last thing I fancied was going somewhere dirty. Basically – I hate being ill, and I just couldn't see the point of packing myself off to certain dysentery and probably worse. I also couldn't figure out what you do all day in a country that's too poor to have museums. Not that I like museums particularly – I just mean that sightseeing's OK for a while – a few weeks, maybe – but what do you do if there aren't any sights? Do you just wander around looking at the poor people and eating disgusting food that ruins your liver for the rest of your life? What do you do all day?

The most eloquent defence of travel I got was from Paul, who said, 'Dunno. There must be *something* to do. Apparently the dope's really cheap.' James had then launched into some enormous long-winded theory about imperialist cultural assumptions and putting yourself into a situation where you're challenged to think about things that are taken for granted in the West, but I could tell that what he actually meant was 'The dope really *is* cheap.' Besides, anyone who talks about challenging their cultural assumptions and then goes to Thailand is clearly talking out of their arse.

Even though I thought the whole thing sounded pretty pointless, I still felt under a certain amount of pressure to do it. However I rationalized my desire to stay in Europe, I always ended up feeling that in all honesty, it came down to cowardice. No other explanation was possible. If I couldn't face going to the Third World, I was a coward.

In the back of my mind, I was hoping that something would happen which would whisk me away to a land of suffering, danger and poverty, but I wasn't willing to make it happen myself. I wanted to have one of those big trips behind me, but I'd never get around to putting myself through it. Suffering, danger and poverty are all fine by me, but dirt and disease are two things I happen to hate. I just didn't want to go.

As for what I'd do when I got back from Switzerland, I felt depressed just thinking about it. I would have earned plenty of money by then, and the obligation to travel would be more powerful than ever. I needed to think of some way to spend it that didn't look like too much of a cop-out.

My job in Switzerland turned out to be just as dull as the one at the Sock Shop, with Alpine boredom differing only from the metropolitan variety in that it is slightly more sweet-smelling. I somehow failed to meet a horny million-airess with months to live, and arrived back in England with no plans as to what I should do with the rest of my year. By now it was March, and all my friends were either abroad or at university.

After repeated desultory flips through my address book, I was forced to acknowledge that something radical had to be done if I wanted to have a life. I dug out the beer-mat and stared at Liz's phone number.

For several days, whenever I passed within reach of a telephone, my pulse accelerated slightly. But I couldn't quite make myself ring her.

After doing the old dial-half-the-number, walk-around-the-house-a-few-times, dial-half-the-number, go-and-buy-some-milk, dial-half-the-number, nip-out-for-a-newspaper, dial-half-the-number, go-into-the-garden-and-torture-a-small-animal routine each day for almost a week, I finally forced myself to go through with it.

'Hello – is Liz there, please?'

'Yup – speaking.'

'Oh.'

I didn't know what to say. What was it you were supposed to say in these situations?

'Hi,' I tried.

That was it. That sounded right.

'Hi. Who is this?'

'Um – it's me. Dave. Dave Greenford. James's friend.'

'Dave! Shit – it's good to hear from you. How's things?'

'Fine, fine.'

'What have you been up to?'

'Oh – this and that. You know. I've just got back from Switzerland.'

'Oh yeah. Of course. How was it?'

'Crap. They're all wankers.'

'Really?'

'Yeah.'

'What – all of them?'

'Everyone I met.'

'God. That's bad luck.'

'Not really – more a statistical certainty.'

'Right. Sounds like you really got into the local culture.'

'Absolutely. Yodelling and rubber cheese – what more could a guy want?'

'You're going back soon, then?'

'Soon as I can. Anyway – what about you? What are you up to?'

'Nothing. I've been bored to piss.'

'Bored to piss? That sounds serious.'

'Everyone's away. All my friends have just vanished off the face of the earth.'

'I'm so pleased to hear you say that. I've got exactly the same problem. It's tragic. Everyone's disappeared. I've been having the social life of a maggot.'

'I would have thought maggots had quite a good social life,' she said. 'I mean, you never see a lonely maggot, do you?'

What a weird thing to say. I felt my cheeks flush. This was it. I was falling in love with her again.

'Make that a maggot with a speech impediment and acne,' I said.

'A wiggle impediment, maybe.'

This was amazing! We were really bonding now.

'Imagine being a maggot with a wiggle impediment,' I said. 'No one would talk to you. If you had, like, half a wiggle, you'd only be able to go round in circles, and everyone would take the piss really badly.'

'Do you reckon there's such a thing as a really sexy, popular maggot? With a curvaceous wiggle?'

I was almost helpless with lust.

'Look – Liz. Are you doing anything?'

'What do you mean?'

'You know – are you up to anything, like, this week?'

'Are you asking me out?'

'No, no, no. I'm not, I'm not. I just . . . sort of wondered if we could sort of meet up for a drink or something.'

'You are. You're asking me out.'

'No – it's nothing like that, I just . . .'

'Stop squirming, you pratt. I'm winding you up. You're James's mate. You're not exactly going to turn round and start groping me the minute he leaves the country, are you?'

I chuckled weakly.

'You two are still going out, then?'

'Of course we are. Look – I've got sod all to do this evening. Do you want to meet in Camden around eight?'

'Right. OK. Cool.'

'I'll see you at the station exit.'

'There's two.'

'At the main one, then.'

'They're the same.'

'Oh, don't be such a knob. I'll see you at the prettier one.'

Then she put the phone down.

Shit! I'd never been bossed around like that before. I

normally spent a good twenty minutes negotiating a suitable meeting place, and she just ... bloody hell! This was amazing.

Another plump, juicy, bursting peach

I was late for our meeting at Camden station, but Liz was even later. I noticed for the first time that one of the exits was marginally less ugly than the other, and that was where she turned up.

We went to the World's End pub, and I ordered a Guinness in the hope that I'd come across as a bit of an intellectual.

It was the first time we'd ever been alone together, and once we'd sat down with our drinks it became clear that we didn't really have very much to talk about. Our only connection was James. I didn't want to encourage her to talk about him, but I didn't want long silences either, and when the first one began to gape open, I chickened out and took the easy option.

'Any news from James?'

'Yeah, lots. He seems to be getting on fine. Got a letter every few days at first, then it started going down. Haven't had one for about a fortnight now.'

'When'd he go?'

'January.'

'Shit – three months.'

'Five more to go.'

'I didn't realize it was that long.'

'Tell me about it.'

'That's a *long* time. Eight months. Don't you reckon he'll get bored?'

'Bored? You think he'll polish off everything there is to do in Thailand, Hong Kong, Bali, Australia and America in eight months, do you?'

'No – it's not that – it's just . . . *eight months* away from home. That's ages. No Marmite. No EastEnders. Warm beer.'

'Warm beer?'

'Apparently, yeah. Except maybe in Australia.'

'I was hoping that he'd be marginally more worried about missing me.'

'Exactly. That too. Eight months . . .'

'It's hard enough already.'

'And you don't mind him running away like that and leaving you alone for all this time?'

'He didn't *run away*. It's his year off for God's sake. I wouldn't want to go out with someone whose idea of fun was sitting in St Albans working as a filing clerk all year.'

'I suppose not. Didn't you want to go with him, though?'

'Of *course* I wanted to go with him. D'you think I'd rather be in a pub with you than on a beach in Thailand with James?'

'No. I suppose not.'

'There is the small matter of my own life to consider. I can't just leave like that. I'm in the middle of a course.'

'Oh yeah. I forgot. Still – he could have waited. I mean, you get a summer holiday, don't you?'

'He's been planning it for years. Since before I even knew him.'

'You don't mind, then?'

'I wouldn't say I don't mind. I'm not exactly over the

moon about being on my own all year. But it's what he's got to do.'

'*Got* to?'

'Yes – got to.'

'Why's he *got* to?'

'Just because he has. That's what he feels.'

'What – so he can *find himself*?'

'You're so cynical about all this. What's your problem?'

'I haven't got a problem. I just don't think . . . you know . . . I don't think he's treating you very well.'

She laughed and shook her head.

'You're funny.'

'Why?' I said, smiling.

'Well – not only are you jealous of him going away, you're also jealous of his girlfriend. And you're supposed to be his mate. I mean, if that's what you think of your *friends* . . .'

That wasn't what I was expecting her to say.

'What do you mean?'

'About what?' She was smirking.

'What do you mean, "jealous of his girlfriend"?'

She spun in her chair, pretending to look around the pub for someone. 'Shit – I think I must mean me,' she said. Then she gave me one of those looks. One of those looks that you have to look away from.

'I don't think you realize what kind of a relationship I have with James,' she said. 'We're not kids any more. This isn't teenagers snogging behind the bike sheds, you know.'

'You're still teenagers.'

'Yes – but we don't snog behind the bike sheds. We make love.'

She said that just to freak me out. There really was no call for that kind of language.

'I'm so impressed.'

'Dave – do you understand what I'm talking about? It's a proper relationship. We're in love.'

'All right, all right, all right, all right. I've got the message. OK. Change of subject – please.'

There was a long silence. I was still avoiding her eyes.

'You know what?' she said.

'What?'

'The funny thing is . . .'

'What?'

'We talked about this before he left.'

'What – about me?'

'No. About *this*.'

'What do you mean?'

'About infidelity.'

'Right.'

'And we decided . . .'

'What?'

'Well – you know. Me and him have been together, what – about five months. Now he's gone away for eight months, and we just thought – that you can't force these things.'

'What things?'

'You know – whatever happens, when he comes back, things aren't going to be the same. We won't be able to just start again where we left off.'

'So . . . ?'

'So, we just thought – that it's better to play things by ear. We both reckoned that with him so far away, for so long, the chances of him – like – behaving himself are really very low, and the more pressure we both feel under to stay – celibate, or something – the harder it will make things. Basically – we both reckon that the more pressure there is, the more likely we are to be unfaithful.'

'What are you saying?'

'Just that . . . we both decided to be a bit open about

things. That if anything happened, it wouldn't be the end of the world. That we should both do what we want.'

'And what *do* you want?'

I was trying to stop myself from smiling.

'Well – I dunno. It's just that me and James – we used to – you know – have a great time. We had an excellent time together. It was *always* great. Well – maybe not at first – I mean, in the beginning he didn't know what the hell he was doing – but once we got going – you know it was always . . . we always had a lot of fun. And up until he left, we were together almost all the time – for weeks. I was virtually living with him. He was always there – and I mean, to be honest . . .' She let out a chuckle. Her cheeks were slightly flushed. 'Look – can I be frank here? To be honest – you get used to it.'

She let that thought sit on the table in front of us, until it was ripe.

'It's only three months, now – and I'm getting – you know . . . almost – like – desperate.'

There was another one. Another plump, juicy, bursting peach. I was very, very excited.

'And . . . ?' I said.

'And what?'

She didn't seem to know what I meant.

'I mean . . . why are you telling me this?'

I gave her a flirtatious look.

'Oh right. I see. Yes – I remember. I was just thinking – that's what's so funny.'

'What? What's funny.'

'You. You're funny.'

'What? Why?'

'It's just funny. You know – the whole thing just seems really ironic.'

'Why?'

'It just makes me laugh. There you are, making these hilariously clumsy passes at me, and if you weren't . . . who you are . . . I'd probably go along with it, just to get it out of my system.'

'What? Who am I? What am I?'

'You're James's mate.'

'So? So what? You happened to meet me through James. So what?'

'So *what?*'

'He's gone. He's not back for ages.'

'Jesus! You might have no scruples, but it makes a difference to me. Besides, it's all wrong, anyway.'

'Why?'

'Well – we're friends, right?'

'Yes.'

'So it's wrong. You know – if you were some guy, and this was the first time I'd met you, we could just – you know – in out thanks very much bye bye. But we're friends. It couldn't work like that.'

'Why not?'

'It just couldn't.'

This was bad news. I pulled my grieving-bloodhound face. Liz let out a half-laugh-half-sigh and gave me a consoling squeeze on the knee. Some consolation *that* was.

'Look – have you forgotten what we said on the phone already?'

'What?'

'All our mates are either out of the country or at university. We're stranded. Look – I'm really glad you've come back from Switzerland. It's great to have someone to hang around with other than the pricks from art college. The two of us can have a laugh together. I wouldn't want to throw that away just for one quick screw.'

43

'Right. I see.'
She patted my thigh.

I would have gladly thrown away just about anything for a quick screw – and who said it would have to be quick, anyway?

Her definition of the word 'desperate' obviously wasn't the same as mine.

Does it have to be India?

In the weeks after our drink in Camden, I saw Liz increasingly often. I began to realize that, in a strange way, she had been right about not shagging.

Because of that conversation, we both knew exactly what the other one thought, and all the sex stuff could be left on one side. I still fancied her, and she knew I still fancied her, but we both knew that nothing was going to happen (or at least acted that way) and as a result, we could become like normal mates.

It was the first time I'd ever had a proper female friend. She really was a good laugh, and it was genuinely possible to get on well with her, despite the fact that I wanted her body but couldn't do anything about it. I actually got on with her better than I could remember getting on with any of my regular friends. We could have a laugh and everything, then, sometimes, if we were in the mood, we had quite serious conversations. I mean, what we ended up saying was occasionally properly . . . well, intimate. I ended up telling her things that I'd never really told anyone before. I can't actually remember what they were now, but at the time I remember thinking that it all felt very deep.

*

Although we were just friends, and I didn't make another pass at her, over time it became obvious that we were getting closer and closer. Whenever we sat down, we always found ourselves *right* next to each other. When we went for walks, we often held hands. And in the cinema, it was quite common for us to squeeze various bits of each other's legs.

Now I'm no expert, but it seemed obvious to me that something sexual was going on. I wasn't making advances to her or anything, but between us, things were just happening – almost of their own accord. And the more we sat around fondling each other, talking about our deepest, darkest secrets and exposing the depths of our hearts to each other, the more there was this massive thing that neither of us was mentioning.

And I knew – you just know when this happens – you do – I just knew that if I had said that we were acting like a pair of honeymooners, she would have acted all shocked, got angry, and the whole thing would have disappeared in a puff of smoke – because if the physical stuff had vanished, the whole friendship would have collapsed almost immediately. We couldn't have gone back to not touching without feeling like complete fakes.

Occasionally, she'd say things like, 'You've got a very close sense of personal space, haven't you?', which is *bollocks* – it's just so wide of the mark. I've got a bigger exclusion zone than Chernobyl, and I hate touching people, I really do – but I'd have to just lie, and tell her that she was right.

She must have known that the whole friendship was a farce, and that something heavy was on the way, but she made damn sure that neither of us could admit it.

I had always assumed that things would come to a head in one sweaty guilt-ridden frenzy, then we'd never be able to talk to each other again. But one day Liz, completely out of the blue, floored me with a suggestion that opened up more sexual possibilities than I had dared dream about.

It was coming to the end of April, and Liz was skiving off college for the third time that week. We had just spent the afternoon lounging around on Hampstead Heath, and both of us were lying on our backs on the ground. I was flat on the grass, and Liz had her head on my belly.

'What are you going to do, then?' she said.

'About what?'

'With the rest of your year.'

'Aaah – that's the five-million-dollar question, isn't it?'

'Six million.'

'It's not that important.'

'You've got over four months left.'

'True.'

'You going to work?'

'Not if I can avoid it.'

'Do you need to work?'

'Not really, no.'

'You're joking.'

'I don't. I'm Mr Moneybags now.'

'Really?'

'Yup. Doesn't it show?'

'No – you're still as tight as ever.'

'Glad to hear it.'

'How come you're so rich, then?'

'Basically – the minimum wage in Switzerland is over a grand a month. And since I didn't have a social life, I saved most of it up.'

'Over a grand a month?'

'Well – they nick back most of your salary in accommodation and food costs – even though they put you up in the cellar and feed you on leftovers from the kitchen. But still – I came back with more than a thousand.'

'Really?'

'Plus what I earned in the Sock Shop.'

'You rich bastard! And have you taken me out for one meal? Have you bought me so much as a lollipop?'

'Look – I'm saving it.'

'What for?'

'For the rest of my year out.'

'So you can travel?'

'Exactly.'

'But you just told me you didn't know what you were going to do.'

'I don't.'

'But you know you're going to travel.'

'Yeah. I suppose so.'

'What do you mean, "You suppose so"? You're acting like I'm persuading you to go away against your will.'

'No.'

'So you do want to travel?'

'I think so.'

'You *think* so.'

'Well – I mean I *want* to. I definitely want to. I'm not scared of it. But I don't . . . I don't want to go on my own, and I haven't really got my arse in gear yet, but everyone else has already left. So I don't really know what to do.'

'I *see*. Right. Blood out of a stone or what?'

There was a silence, while Liz stared out over London, thinking.

'I've got a long summer holiday, you know,' she said. 'I break up in early June. That would give us three months.'

'Are you being serious?'

'Deadly serious. I don't want to be left out of all this, just because I'm doing an art foundation. And I'm not going

48

to trot after James and join up with him in America either.'
She looked at me and broke into a smile. 'I've always
wanted to go to India, you know.'

'India?'

'I've got some savings. Do you want to go to India with
me? This summer?'

'Are you serious?'

'I'm on for it if you are.'

'Does it have to be India? Couldn't we do Australia?'

'I'm not wasting my money on that. It's India or nothing.'

I thought for less than one second, a vision popping into
my head of a spartan hotel room with a marble floor, a
ceiling fan, and Liz and me fucking like bunny rabbits on
a huge double bed.

'All right,' I said.

'Shake on it.'

We shook on it.

Just touching her hand like that turned me on. Liz and
I were going abroad together for the whole summer. Sharing
hotel rooms. There was no way, given the circumstances,
that I could possibly fail to shag her.

She gripped my hand, and gave me one of her stares. 'As
mates,' she said. 'It's only going to work if that's absolutely
clear.'

'Fine. As mates,' I said, leaning forward to give her a
peck on the cheek.

The hot, wet gusset of James's boxer shorts

Liz's dad agreed to pay for her ticket, on condition that he met me first. I was duly invited to her parents' house for dinner, along with my mum and dad. This turned out to be one of the most stagnant social occasions I had ever attended. If an alien had landed in the room, he would have thought that human beings communicate by clanking cutlery together. Still, I seemed to fulfil whatever criteria he had in mind, and he gave her the money.

Liz and I started spending whole days together, poring over maps, flipping through guidebooks, and gradually planning a route. We would fly to Delhi, head north to the Himalayas, do a little loop into Rajasthan, then head south to Bombay, Goa, and right down to Kerala at the very bottom. After that we'd go back up the other side from Madras to Calcutta, across to Varanasi, north to Kathmandu, then back to Delhi to fly home. The middle of the country is apparently really boring – just loads of people growing food and getting hot, so doing a loop around the edge was the best route to avoid missing anything.

A lot of these planning sessions went on late into the night, and I occasionally slept at her place. This was a cramped student house which she shared with three other girls from her course, and there was no spare bedroom, so I had to sleep on a few cushions on her floor. There was something deeply erotic about this. Lying there chatting, after we'd switched the lights out, felt almost like pillow talk. A serenely post-coital atmosphere hung in the air, only marginally spoilt by the fact that I usually had a screaming hard-on.

Once, we'd already been pillow-talking for some time, when she told me that she had a stiff neck.

'Would you like a massage?' I said.

'Are you any good?'

'All right,' I said, meaning, 'Never done one before in my life, but I'll give it a go.'

She turned round to lie on her front, and I climbed up to her bed, pushed aside her duvet, and started squeezing the back of her neck.

At first she lay there giving me all the reasons why she had a stiff neck that day, and telling me how James was an excellent masseur. She went on and on about him, so I switched off and stopped listening. As I gradually figured out how to do it, I noticed that her speech slowed down, and the gaps between her sentences got longer and longer, until the gaps were winning.

Then she started making these noises. I don't think I can actually call them moans. That would be overstating things. They didn't quite qualify as moans, and they weren't exactly sighs – they were kind of hums-plus-a-bit.

Soon I wasn't just doing her neck; I was doing her shoulders and the top of her back. Then I started catching my fingers in the neck of her T-shirt – trying to give the impression that it was getting in the way and making a real massage impossible.

It was an odd scene, really. There I was, dressed only in a pair of boxer shorts, sitting astride her, massaging her back, while she hummed-plus-a-bit, and every few minutes told me what good mates we were, and how much she loved James.

I began to inch her T-shirt upwards until it was gathered around her armpits. Under cover of doing an upper-arm, forearm and hand massage, I straightened her arms out above her head. Then, in a gentle swoop, the T-shirt came over her head, down her arms, and on to the floor.

Whoosh!

I smoothed her hair back in place, and looked at her back.

Her long, sweeping, elegant, gorgeous back.

Now, without the T-shirt in the way, I could sweep, slide and rub in long, easy, unimpeded movements.

She stopped talking, and the hums-plus-a-bit turned into moans.

At the side of her back, I could feel the bulge of her tits. They were right there, uncovered, pressed into the sheet. And I was right there with them.

After a while, I moved down and started on her legs. On the way past, I noticed that all she was wearing was a pair of men's boxer shorts.

Now she was definitely moaning. Up and down I went, over her whole body, my hands subtly slipping into the pant area on the way past. One of these little explorations flipped over the elastic on her boxer shorts, revealing, of all things, a name-tag. In the half-light bleeding through the curtains from a street lamp, I could just make out the words. 'JAMES IRVING', it said.

I snapped the elastic back into place.

Gradually, I started focusing my attention on her thighs, then on the inside of her thighs, then on the top of the inside of her thighs. In a series of tiny adjustments, her legs parted, accommodating my hand.

Slowly, her hips rose a fraction from the mattress. I followed the invitation, and found my fingers in the hot, wet gusset of James's boxer shorts. After this, I just held firm and watched. I hardly needed to move. Her hips rocked back and forwards over my hand, gradually faster and harder, until she made this funny squeaky noise, had a little shudder, then pushed my hand away, rolled over and fell asleep.

Instead of going back to my bed, I curled up behind her and tried to doze off, with my erection pressed firmly into her bum.

In the morning I was the first to wake up, so I crawled to my bed and woke up again there, in order to do my bit for the illusion that nothing had happened. Having done that, I went downstairs, made two breakfasts, and took them back to the bedroom. I balanced the tray on Liz's clock-radio, and got into bed with her. She was still half asleep, but had somehow conveniently put her T-shirt on.

Together we chomped through our cereal and toast like two good mates who just happened to be having a companionable breakfast on the same mattress. Neither of us mentioned what had happened, even though with every mouthful I took, I noticed a thrillingly salty odour on my fingers.

Later that week, Liz and I bought our tickets. We would leave immediately after the end of her term, and return almost three months later, just in time for me to start university.

Not now having sex

After a while, sleep-overs with massage became a regular occurrence. The massage technique gradually developed until it involved both of us stripping down to our pants and rubbing different bits of our bodies together.

Since Liz never raised the topic of our burgeoning sexual relationship in conversation, I decided to play along with her and let us continue with the illusion that we were two good mates who just happened to have a fondness for near-nude medicinal massage. The healing properties of this massage gradually found themselves focused more and more on the genitals, at which point underwear became a bigger inconvenience than ever, and suddenly we were naked.

It is a well-known fact that if two people lie in bed, without clothes, rubbing each other's genitals together, sooner or later, one genital will slot into the other.

This is what happened. A *very* advanced form of medicinal massage.

It was at this point that we chose to discuss contraception.

'You're on the Pill, aren't you?'

'No. I stopped.'

'Have you got any condoms?'

'No. I threw my spares away.'

'Why?'

'As a gesture.'

'For fuck's sake! A gesture of what?'

'Fidelity, of course.'

'Oh, right.'

'You'd better pull out.'

'All right.'

'NOT YET, you idiot.'

'Oh, OK.'

I wiggled my dick around a bit, until it started to tingle, then pulled out.

'Will you toss me off?'

'No!'

'Go on. Please.'

'Why should I?'

'I've done you loads of times, and you've never even touched me.'

She scowled, and reached under the duvet. Having somehow found the only part of my penis without any nerve endings, she tugged it until it ached. Cradling her hand, I showed her what to do, and within seconds, I had squirted on to her belly.

It was, I feel I must stress, only the semen of friendship. A form of natural massage oil, if you will. For there was nothing sexual between Liz and me. Absolutely not. Further proof of this can be found in the fact that she *still* refused to kiss me.

Afterwards we both went to sleep, probably more out of tact than anything else. I knew she'd need time to decide what to say. It would now be very hard indeed for her to deny that something had happened. With any luck, we'd wake up the next morning, have a bad-breath kiss and officially name ourselves lovers.

*

The second Liz opened her eyes, she leaped out of bed. I followed her downstairs, and we had breakfast in silence until I popped the big question.

'Liz? Why won't you kiss me?'

She carried on eating, staring into her cereal bowl and chewing slowly while she decided on an answer.

'Isn't it obvious?' she mumbled.

'In the circumstances, nothing seems very obvious at all.'

'I don't love you,' she said.

'So?'

'What do you mean, "so"?'

'I know you don't love me. I know where we stand. It's just that if we're going to . . . you know . . . have sex, then we might as well try and enjoy it.'

'I love James. Doesn't that mean anything to you?'

'Not much. Look – it's ridiculous that you keep on about him while you're doing all this stuff with me. I don't see why you can't just acknowledge what's going on – then, when he gets back, we can all return to normal.'

'Is that really what you want?'

'Of course.'

'And you think things work like that, do you?'

'I don't see why not. We could always give it a go.'

'You are so naïve. I find it hard to believe that you can know so little about relationships. You're talking shit.'

'Why? What would go wrong? You think I wouldn't be able to let go?'

'Yes.'

'I'd be fine. If I've agreed in advance, then I won't be able to complain, will I?'

'And there is the small matter of James. Have you never heard of a thing called jealousy? I don't think he'd be exactly over the moon.'

'I thought you agreed to have an open relationship so

that he could screw around in Asia without feeling bad. It serves him right.'

'I don't believe you. I don't know why we're even discussing this. You're just so naïve that I don't know where to start. You don't seem to know anything. And I'm not just a piece of meat that you two can trade between you.'

'We're the ones that are being traded. You've traded him in for me.'

'No I haven't.'

'Of course you have.'

'I have not. If . . . if you feel that just because you have clawed away at me, preying on the fact that you know I miss James . . . and now that you have finally got some pathetic piece of gratification for your efforts – if you think this means you have taken James's place, then you've got a lot to learn.'

'Like what?'

'Like . . . like . . . *everything*. You don't seem to know a single thing about how relationships work. It's as if you've never heard of human emotions. It's as if you haven't even got the imagination to realize that what happens on the surface isn't always the sum total of . . . isn't always the most important thing.'

'Oh, *right*. I *see*. I'm superficial because I think that having sex means something. At last I understand. It's all *my fault* for making the . . . the *naïve* assumption that because you are now having sex with me instead of James . . .'

'I am *not* now having sex with you instead of James. Look – you've been groping me for long enough, and you've finally got your way, and I hope you're satisfied, but now it's going to stop.'

'Great. And I'm the superficial one.'

'Yes.'

'Look. Even if you stop doing it we both know that you want it. We both know that we've done it.'

'I *don't* want it.'

'Yeah, right. I forced you.'

'You did.'

'WHAT ARE YOU TALKING ABOUT?'

'You did. You forced me. Over a matter of weeks, you have gradually forced yourself on me.'

'That's bollocks.'

'It's true. I don't know how you can deny it.'

'I didn't force it to happen. It just happened. And I didn't notice you resisting.'

'If I haven't been resisting, why didn't it happen straight away?'

'Maybe *I* didn't want it to happen.'

'Yeah, that's likely. You'd shag anything.'

'You're really flattering yourself, here.'

'Anyway – we haven't had sex. There *is* a difference between wanking on to someone's belly and making love.'

'It was your hand.'

'My hand was limp. You were moving it for me, if you don't remember.'

'And you've forgotten what happened before that, have you?'

'Oh yeah – you dabbed your weenie at me for about ten seconds. Wow. That's what I call passion. I've never had it so good.'

'If you'd had some condoms . . .'

'But I didn't. For precisely this reason.'

'If you hadn't been afraid that we were going to make love, you wouldn't have had to throw them away.'

'We did *not* make love, and we're never going to. If that's your idea of love-making, then you've had a *very* sad life indeed.'

'Oh, fuck off.'

'And I hope I've answered your question. That's why I won't kiss you. Because you're a fucking prick.'

Nothing much

It was a week before I summoned the courage to give her a ring.

'Hi,' I said. 'It's me.'

'Hi.'

'What are you up to?'

'Nothing much.'

'Shall I come over?'

'No. I'm busy.'

'I thought you said you were doing nothing much.'

'Yes – but I'm about to do something, aren't I?'

'What?'

'None of your business.'

'Fair enough.'

There was an awkward silence.

'Shall I come over later?'

'No – I told you. I'm busy.'

'But I'm not allowed to ask what you're doing?'

'Look – I've got a lot of work to catch up on. I don't want to fail my course, you know.'

'What about after that, though? Shouldn't we do a bit more planning?'

'Don't be ridiculous. We already know exactly where we're going. We've decided as much as we can decide. You can't control everything, you know. If we try and plan anything else we're just going to kill the whole thing dead.'

Given that I had used the word 'planning' as a euphemism for sex (possibly a linguistic first), her answer was a very bad sign.

'I'm fed up of planning,' she said, ramming the message home. 'We've decided what we're going to do, and we should just leave the rest until we get there. You're far too anal – you know that? You can't decide everything in advance for your whole life.'

I didn't know what to say. This is it, I thought to myself. I've blown it, and we haven't even got to India yet.

'Look – I've got to get on,' she said.

'OK.'

'Bye.'

Click.

'Bye.'

She put the phone down before I even said 'bye'.

There were only three days left before our departure. In that time, we didn't speak.

PART TWO

What do backpackers do all day?

The Book

On our first full day in Delhi we went to the Red Fort, which was enormous and impressive but fundamentally a bit boring. A guy just outside was selling floppy hats with a brim all the way round, wearing a huge pile of them on his head as a crowd-pulling technique. The sight of him made me realize that I felt as if someone had been dropping bricks on my head. I needed one of those hats.

'Hello, friend. You buy hat?'

'How much?'

'Best price.'

'How much?'

'What you like.'

'What *I* like?'

'You give price.'

'How much are they normally?'

'You give price, friend. Any price – cheap price.'

'Um . . . fifty rupees?'

This was just under two quid, which seemed reasonable to me, but the instant I said it he plonked a hat on my head and waited for me to pay. I'd obviously offered far too much, but I didn't really see how I could go about changing my mind, so I gave him the cash.

Liz, pretending that she hadn't seen what happened, asked me what I had paid and laughed in my face. I said I didn't care, and thought it was a perfectly fair price for what I had got, since it was a very cool hat.

'Haven't you noticed that every other Westerner in the city is wearing one? You might as well walk around carrying a placard saying "Tourist".'

I looked around to see if what she had said was true. A group of thirty middle-aged Europeans with a tour guide emerged from the fort. More than half of them were wearing my hat.

'Where's your tour guide, Dave? Aren't you going to join your friends?'

'Look – this isn't a fashion parade, Liz. It feels comfortable, so I'm happy. If you want to get sunstroke just so you don't look like a tourist, that's your problem.'

'I am going to buy a hat. I just might not buy it from the first guy I see in front of the biggest tourist spot in the capital city. Personally, I'd rather be just that little bit unobtrusive.'

'Great idea. A hat's really going to do the trick. What else are you going to do? Put shoe polish on your face?'

'Racist.'

I wished I hadn't bought the hat now, but thanks to the argument I'd have to wear it all the time, just to show that she hadn't changed my mind.

I did wonder how much everyone else had paid for it, though.

Jeremy had told us that the rickshaw to and from the fort shouldn't cost more than ten rupees each way (roughly thirty pence). Our attempts to get this price were met by the rickshaw drivers with derision. Liz managed to respond to their prices with equal, if not greater derision, and I ended up spectating on twenty-minute arguments in both directions. At regular intervals, either Liz or the driver marched off in a huff, and when it was Liz's turn, I felt honour-bound to follow her.

Liz managed to get the trip for fifteen going and twenty coming back, both of which she considered to be significant moral victories. Huddled in the back of the noisy, stinking rickshaw, I could tell that she expected some kind of approval for her labours.

'Well done, Liz.'

'Thanks.'

'You saved us at least 15p there. That's almost 8p each.'

'Will you stop acting like such a spoilt Westerner? We're in India, now.'

'So?'

'So you have to haggle. It's part of life.'

'You don't have to. Stump up a few extra pennies, and you don't need to stand in the midday sun screaming your head off like some deranged memsahib.'

'It's not about that, and you know it.'

'What is it about, then?'

'Look – if you just take the first price they offer, you look stupid. They laugh at you behind your back.'

'So? Who cares?'

'And if Westerners go around paying double for everything, it gives us a bad reputation. It sets a bad example. It makes us all look spoilt, and far richer than we really are.'

'But we *are* rich. Ten rupees is nothing. It doesn't matter if we pay double.'

'That's not the point. If we did that, it would completely upset the local economy.'

'Oh, right. I *see*. It's like the beggars all over again. There

I was, thinking you were being tight-fisted, and it turns out you're selflessly doing battle for the good of the local economy.'

'I'm getting very bored of this pseudo-worldly sarcasm crap, Dave. It's got nothing to do with being tight-fisted. I'm just not going to let those people make me look like an idiot.'

'And you looked really sensible giving yourself a haemorrhage over twenty pence.'

'Oh, sod off.'

We were stopped at a junction by a traffic policeman, and a pair of child beggars tapped on the side of the rickshaw, then stuck their heads pleadingly inside. Liz fished around in her money belt for coins, presumably to demonstrate that she wasn't stingy. Both myself and the beggar watched her fiddle with the money belt, which now contained a wad of notes almost half an inch thick. I saw the child's eyes widen with awe.

'I haven't got any coins,' said Liz.

The rickshaw driver revved his engine. Liz flicked through her banknotes, frantically searching for a low denomination.

'Can you give him something?'

'I thought . . .'

'DON'T START,' she snapped, with impressive venom. Her fuse had obviously been considerably shortened by her arguments with the rickshaw men. And by her lack of a hat.

Just then, the driver turned and swore at the beggar in Hindi. The beggar ignored him, sensing that he was close to getting some money.

The driver carried on shouting at the child while I fished in my pocket for a coin. Just as the traffic began to move,

I found one and put it in the child's hand as we pulled away. His wrist was knocked by the rickshaw, and I saw the coin fly out.

Spinning round to look out of the back, I saw the child on his knees in the middle of the road, oblivious to the traffic which was hooting and swerving, inches away from smashing into him. As he receded into the distance, I saw the other beggar join the search of the Tarmac, and the beginnings of a scuffle when one of them picked up the coin.

Back at the hotel, Jeremy was sitting on the veranda, reading.

'You made it?' he said.

'Just about,' I answered.

'How much did you pay for the rickshaw?' he said.

Liz jumped in before I could answer. 'Fifteen.'

'And twenty on the way back,' I said.

'Not bad,' said Jeremy. 'Bit more practice and you'll be there.'

'What are you reading?' said Liz.

'The *Gita*,' he said, holding up a copy of the *Bhagavad Gita*.

'Oh, wow,' said Liz.

'Is it any good?' I said.

He gave me a patronizing look. 'Good? This is the *Gita* we're talking about, here. I mean, is the bible any "good"?' He made the inverted commas with his fingers.

'Dunno. I've never read it. I expect it's got a few good bits.'

He turned to Liz, ostentatiously addressing his comments away from me.

'It is *the* book. It explains everything you need to know about India. You can't come here and not read it.'

'I thought the Lonely Planet was *the* book. Is the *Bhagavad Gita* better than the Lonely Planet, then? Are the prices more up-to-date?'

They both ignored me.

'Can I borrow it after you've finished?' said Liz.

He chuckled.

'You never finish the *Bhagavad Gita*. I've been through it more times than I can remember. Here.' He closed the book, and threw it to her. It wasn't a very good throw, but she managed to catch it, and looked at him, slightly bewildered. He smiled back. 'From me,' he said. 'Call it an introductory gift. To India.' He put his arms behind his head, leaned back in his chair, and stared at the ceiling. 'Maybe, if you feel like it, at some point you'll give me one of your books.'

In return for his sixty-page, dog-eared copy of the *Bhagavad Gita*, he got a fresh, unread *Oscar and Lucinda*.

'We've decided what to do,' said Liz.

'Oh?' said Jeremy.

'We're going to stick to our original plan. It's just too hot down here, and the monsoon's on the way, so we're going to head for the mountains. We reckon Simla's a good place for a first stop.'

'Simla?'

'D'you reckon that sounds like a good idea?'

'You've got to do what feels right for you, Liz. I can't tell you where to go.'

'What – is there something wrong with Simla?'

'Go where the feeling takes you, Liz. That's what you're here for. There's no right or wrong.'

'I didn't mean that. I only . . .'

'Just go. Chill out.'

'D'you want to . . . come with us?'

70

NO! No – she couldn't ask that. Not Jeremy. I couldn't face it.

'I'd love to,' he said.

Noooo.

'But I can't.'

'Why not?' said Liz. 'I thought you could go where the feeling took you.'

'Nice one. I just can't. I'm stuck here, waiting for some money to come through.'

'Waiting for some money to come through?' I said.

'Yeah. I've run out.'

'Where's it coming from?' I said.

'Home.'

'How come? From who?'

'Parents.'

I couldn't stop myself from laughing. That's the life, I thought. Mummy and daddy cabling you money whenever you ran out.

'What?' he said. 'What's funny?'

'Nothing.'

'What are you laughing at?'

'*Nothing*. Am I laughing? Is this a laugh?'

'You were laughing. I want to know what you were laughing at.'

'Just . . . you know.'

'No, I don't know.'

'Just – it's funny that your parents send you money.'

'Why?'

'It just is.' I smirked. I'd really got under his skin now. 'I just – you know – took you for someone a bit older, that's all.'

He stood up, throwing *Oscar and Lucinda* on to the ground.

'What do you mean by that?'

'Nothing.'

The atmosphere thickened as we stared at each other, neither of us speaking.

'I'm sorry,' I said. 'I shouldn't have laughed. I mean – just because I earned the money to come here doesn't make me any better than you. And it wasn't really a surprise anyway. I shouldn't have laughed. It was obvious from when you first opened your mouth that you were a toff. I'm sorry. I shouldn't have laughed.'

He was really pissed off now.

'I am *not* a toff.'

'No – sorry. Wrong word.'

'And I *did* earn the money to come here. My parents just happen to be sending me a top-up.'

'Right. Exactly. I'm leaping to conclusions.'

'And I am *not* a toff.'

'Sorry. Touchy subject.'

He was twitching with rage.

'People like you . . . people . . . it's your kind of . . . of . . . *obsession* with class that . . . that really . . . it's so juvenile, and so English. You're just so fucking *English* it makes me sick. You're narrow-minded, and pathetic – and you don't know *anything* about me. So bugger off.'

'You're right. Let's get to know each other better, shall we? Like – what school did you go to?'

'I bet you went to private school, too.'

'Maybe I did, but that doesn't make me a toff.'

'I am NOT a . . . a bloody . . .' If he hadn't been a wimp, he would have hit me. I saw it cross his mind. Instead he took a few deep breaths, picked up his book, and stormed off into the hotel. In the doorway, he turned round and shouted at me, 'I hope you . . . I hope you . . . get malaria.'

A sadist's zero-gravity chamber

Liz showed Jeremy our bus tickets to Simla. He kindly pointed out that seats 52 and 53 were going to be at the back, and that it's basic knowledge to make sure that you get a seat near the front if you don't want to have your spine shattered by the bumps in the road. He also mentioned that our tickets said 'Luxury VT' on them, which meant that the bus had a video and we would be deafened by Hindi musicals for the entire journey, which, he gleefully added, took at least fourteen hours.

'How long were you queuing?' he said.

We both scowled at him.

'Two hours,' said Liz.

'You should have got the hotel to send a boy for you,' said Jeremy.

'Do they really do that?' said Liz.

'Of course – costs a few rupees, but it saves you a day. Oh well – live and learn.'

More than ever, I wanted to pull out Jeremy's toenails.

It turned out that the stuff about shattering your spine wasn't just a turn of phrase. The rear wheels of the bus were roughly half-way down the chassis, turning the back fifteen rows into a pivot which magnified the slightest bump in what was already a staggeringly uneven road. As a result, we travelled in a kind of sadist's zero-gravity chamber, where you spent half the time floating in mid air and the other half having your arse spanked by the seat.

It was the first time I had got close to a local for any length of time, and it struck me that all the stuff about Indians accepting their fate was true. The guy next to me didn't even seem to notice how uncomfortable the bus was. Occasionally, if we'd just floated to the ceiling and then been given a triple-whack which was hard enough to send all five of us on to the floor, he would give me an isn't-this-funny grin, but other than that, he just stared out of the window, seemingly content that he was being simultaneously paralysed and castrated.

The one advantage of being at the back was that you were further away from the Hindi musicals playing at the front of the bus. In the course of the trip, the same film was played four times, and although I could only see the screen when I was in mid air, by the end of the journey I'd watched most of the film piecemeal, and could just about follow the story.

As far as I could tell it was about a guy who wants to marry a sexy girl, but his parents want him to marry an ugly girl. Just when he's about to marry the ugly girl, he discovers that the sexy girl has been kidnapped by an ugly man who wears black leather and scowls at the camera. The hero rushes out on a horse in search of the kidnapped sexy girl, and has a punch-up in the desert with the ugly man. He's about to save the sexy girl when it emerges that the ugly girl is in cahoots with the ugly man, and she has somehow tied the father to a chair in the sand and is in the process of pouring petrol all over him. The ugly girl pulls out a box of matches, and they all pause to sing a song. Just then, fifty blokes in black jump out from behind a bush that wasn't there until they jumped out from behind it and start shooting at the hero, who hides behind a small wooden box. Eventually, he comes out, holding a white handkerchief, but when the ugly man in black comes to gloat (which he does in song) the hero trips him up, steals his gun, and shoots all the fifty men in black who jumped out from behind the magically appearing bush.

The father, whose petrol seems to have dried off, frees himself from the chair and has a comedy fight with a fat man who appears to serve no purpose. The sexy girl points out to the hero that the ugly girl is escaping through the desert just as the father defeats the fat man by putting a bucket on his head. The hero, the father and the sexy girl then all sing a song in which the father seems to give his blessing to their marriage. Meanwhile, the ugly girl on the horizon shakes her fist, and says something which can only be a vow of revenge. A few seconds later, just as she is on the point of dying of thirst, she comes across a lonely hut on top of a sand-dune. She knocks on the door and is welcomed by a man who tries to seduce her (in song). She is unimpressed by his advances until she notices that in the corner of the room is a mini-laboratory, containing what appears to be a half-finished nuclear bomb. Together they hatch a plan.

After that, the plot became a bit too difficult to follow. As far as I could tell, in the end the sexy people married each other, the ugly people got blown up, and the fat people ended up with buckets on their head.

Now that's what I call quality entertainment.

The journey included plenty of stops where everyone got out and drank glasses of tea which was sweeter than Coke, and only marginally less milky than milk. At first it made me gag, but as the trip progressed I gradually got into it as a drink. The secret was to avoid thinking of it as tea. As long as you persuaded yourself that it was a warmed-up soft drink, the taste was OK. And it gave you enough of a sugar rush to restore your will to live after several hours of arse-spanking.

There was only one other Westerner on the bus, and despite the fact that he had the best seat, right at the front, he seemed distinctly miserable. Every time we stopped, he was the first one out of the bus, hitting the ground at a sprint, and dashing off, clutching a loo roll.

Liz struck up a conversation with him at one of the stops, but when I noticed that his shirt was flecked with vomit I decided to steer clear. It turned out that he was Belgian and had blood in his stool, so we both avoided him after that.

We discovered that lunch was included in the price of the ticket when someone plonked a cardboard tray filled with unidentifiable blobs of curry on our laps. I waited for Liz to try each blob before I had a go, but I only really trusted the yellow blob, which I could tell was made of lentils. In one corner was a tub of unidentifiable white stuff which had set into a firmish lump with a smooth surface. The guy on my left saw me poke at it and said, 'Crrd'.

'What?'

'Crrd.'

'I don't understand.'

'Crrd.' He took a spoonful. 'Very good.'

'Liz, what's crrd?'

'It's that white stuff.'

'I know, but what is it?'

'I don't know.'

'Are you going to try it?'

'Don't see why not.'

She tasted a large floppy lump.

'It's nice. Kind of like yoghurt.'

'Bloody hell – I'm not touching that.'

'Please yourself.'

She ate the whole of hers, swearing that it was delicious, but I thought she was mad. After all, yoghurt's basically off milk, isn't it? It's insane to put all that effort into an against-the-odds struggle to avoid eating disease-infested food, and then deliberately shovel rancid dairy products into your mouth. No way.

The rest of the journey took twice as long as I had expected, and if it hadn't been for the fact that random people kept on appearing out of nowhere and selling bananas and nuts through the window, I would have starved.

A few strategic apologies

By the time we got to Simla, I'd eaten so many bananas that I already had the shits, despite the fact that I'd only eaten two curries so far on the entire trip.

Liz found it hilarious that I'd given myself a bad tummy by avoiding curry, which I took as a symptom of the worsening vibe that seemed to be developing between us. Once, on the bus, I tried to clear the air by venting my anger over the fact that she had invited Jeremy to come with us, but it didn't really work. She just got all het up, and ranted on about how we didn't own the bus, and we didn't own Simla, and it was always nice to travel with a bit of company. I couldn't help feeling as if this meant that I didn't count as company any more, which also seemed like a bad sign.

Simla was reasonably nice, and we spent a few days wandering around, looking at each of the sights mentioned in The Book. Even though there were far fewer beggars than in Delhi, and we generally got hassled far less, I still couldn't get rid of the feeling that I was shit-scared of everyone and everything. Even people who weren't shouting at us to buy or sell things frightened me. Just that I'm-poor-and-you're-rich look in their eyes made me feel depressed and guilty.

Worst of all were the kids, who swarmed around you asking what your name was, or for a pen, or sometimes for money. They jumped at you constantly, ambushing you just when you were least expecting it, screaming questions at you, and waving their grubby little fingers towards you in the hope that you'd give them a handshake. The kids were usually so dirty I hated having to touch them, but they'd never go away until you had at least patted them on the head.

Liz seemed to enjoy being mobbed by lice-infested street urchins and often squatted down to talk or play with them, while I hovered at a safe distance. As far as I could tell, she had no understanding whatsoever of the means by which disease is transmitted. Either that or she fancied herself as a Mother Teresa.

My personal space was so perpetually invaded by the children, the salesmen and the general crowds that I realized I either had to give up on the idea of having one, or embark on a nervous breakdown. For the time being, it seemed as if the latter was the easier option, and every morning I woke up feeling mildly sick at the thought that there was only breakfast between my bed and the outside world.

I found myself staring at other travellers, to try and tell whether they were genuinely having a good time or were only pretending. Some of them were quite blatantly having a shit time, but if I spotted a group who looked happy, I found myself watching them intently and eavesdropping on them, to try and figure out how they could possibly be having fun.

I failed to see how anyone could enjoy being in India. How did they do it? What was wrong with them? Or was I simply weak-willed and over-sensitive? Maybe I'd been right in thinking that I was too much of a coward to deal with the Third World. Perhaps I should have been honest with myself, and spent the money on a month in Benidorm?

I decided to try and cheer myself up by sending a couple of postcards home.

Dear Mum & Dad,

We arrived safely a few days ago and are already up in the mountains. As you can see from the front, Simla is in an amazing setting, right up in the mountains, with bizarre English-looking houses and even a church! There's incredible poverty everywhere, but I think I might be getting used to it. I'm staying in the YMCA, where there's a full-size snooker table with a little ivory plaque on the side commemorating Major Thompson, who got a break of 109 here in 1902. Hope you're well.

love,
Dave

Dear Grandad,

Greetings from India! It's really hot here, but I'm having an amazing time. Haven't been here long, but I can already tell what an amazing country it is. The roads are really bad, though. Hope you're well.

love,
Dave

I could tell that Liz was as miserable as me, but neither of us wanted to talk about it, so we soldiered on, trying to enjoy Simla. After a few days, we'd seen all the main things and felt that we had recovered enough from the previous bus journey to embark on another one, this time taking us further up into the mountains to the small town of Manali. Everyone we met told us that Manali was the place to be – apparently, it was a kind of Goa-in-the-hills. This would be a perfect place to relax and to give ourselves a little breathing space. So far, everything had just been too hectic.

The mountains on the way to Manali were spectacular, but the town itself looked grim at first sight. Still, we had

Jeremy's recommendation for a peaceful out-of-town hotel called the Rainbow Lodge and headed there on foot, following an impossible-to-follow map in The Book.

We were accompanied most of the way by touts from various hotels who tried to drag us off in different directions and refused to direct us to the one we wanted, insisting that the Rainbow Lodge was overpriced and dirty, and begging us to take a quick look at their hotel. They were so insistent that you had to hate them, while at the same time feeling guilty because they all looked piss-poor, and their hotels probably weren't any worse than the Rainbow Lodge, and it wouldn't have been very difficult to go five minutes out of our way to at least have a glance. Still, if you went around caving in to all the pressure you'd go mad. You have to stand firm and do what you want. If you show any weakness or sympathy, they'll fuck you over.

By the time we found the hotel, we were both feeling stressed and knackered. Still, at least we'd seen the town, which meant we'd got all the tourism done in advance, and could settle in for some serious puffing. By all accounts, this was *the best* hotel in Manali for dope, and having taken a room, we installed ourselves excitedly on the veranda. Within seconds, a joint had found its way into our hands.

I sucked the smoke deeply into my lungs and held my breath, exhaling slowly through my nose at the last possible moment. After a few drags, I felt my anxiety begin to fade.

Now this was more like it. A peaceful place, surrounded by fields, with mountains to look at, and drugs to smoke. *This* made sense. At last we had found a place where you could chill out and concentrate on enjoying yourself. Passing a joint between us, for the first time since we had landed Liz and I smiled at each other.

I didn't want to scrounge too much dope, so I asked the guy next to me where I could buy some.

'Yeah,' he smiled, 'that's right.' Then he nodded wisely. A few seconds later, he realized that he hadn't answered me yet and nodded towards the reception desk. 'Ronnie's your main man,' he said, then he slapped me on the shoulder affectionately and fell off his chair.

At reception I asked if Ronnie was around. The receptionist reached under the desk and pulled out a large lunch-box with the name Ronnie and a happy face painted on it, in dribbly yellow paint.

He opened the box and passed me a cling-film wrapper full of grass.

'One hundred and fifty rupees,' he said, and I paid him.

This was fantastic! A bag of real grass, worth about fifty quid in England, had set me back less than a fiver. India, all of a sudden, seemed like the most civilized country on earth.

I went and got some Rizlas from my backpack. (The Book says you can't get Rizlas in India, so we'd brought an industrial-sized family mega-pack of them.) Joining Liz again on the veranda, I skinned up.

Now we were really smiling at each other. It struck me, for the first time since leaving England, that I was in possession of a penis. I felt the beginnings of a rekindling libido, and decided to embark on a few strategic apologies.

'Liz – I'm sorry, you know.'

'About what?'

'Just . . . everything.'

She smiled at me.

'I've been – you know – behaving like a bit of an arsehole. Everything's just freaked me out,' I said.

'It's OK.'

'Now we're here, I think things can calm down a bit.'

'I hope so.'

'Let's try and get on, yeah?'

'OK.'

'Both of us,' I said, pointedly. I'd only really apologized in the hope that it would make *her* apologize. After all, she was the one really acting the arsehole, not me.

'All right. We'll both try and be a bit nicer to each other, then.'

That didn't really qualify as an apology in my book, but at least it came with a genuine smile, so after a brief consultation with my ever-swelling dick, I decided to accept it as a peace-offering.

I reached out my hand and smiled back.

'Bygones?' I said.

'Bygones.'

She took my hand.

'We're stuck with each other now, so we might as well make an effort,' I said, giving her hand a little squeeze.

'I think we can get on,' she said, squeezing back.

The joint went backwards and forwards between us a few times, with our hands remaining interlocked. Veins in my drought-stricken groin started singing joyous blood-worshipping anthems.

While she sucked out the last of the smoke, I reached over and stroked the back of her hand. We remained like this for a good while, staring in amicable silence at the staggeringly beautiful view of the Himalayas: lush foothills, with every curve shaped into a paddy-field, topped by enormous snowy peaks. I had never seen anything so impressive.

Yes – at last – I was pleased to be in India. I could feel the knot of tension in my stomach beginning to loosen. Paul and James had been right about travel, after all. This was an amazing experience. And the dope really was cheap.

'Shall I roll another?' I said, eventually.

'Why not?'

She blinked at me, slowly.

'Shall we have a smoke in the room?'

'OK.'

Still hand in hand, we shuffled inside.

She sat on the bed, while I locked the door and drew the curtains. I slid on to the bed next to her, and we stared at each other, half-smirks playing on our mouths.

'Can't just sit here all day,' I said. 'I've got work to do.'

She raised an eyebrow at me, and I answered her by plucking out a few Rizlas. I licked and stuck them together, while Liz settled back against the headboard. With the joint completed, I sat next to her, placed it in her hand and extended the lighter.

'Would Madame care to commence?'

She grinned, and planted the joint droopily into the corner of her mouth. I lit it for her, enjoying the way her eyes narrowed when she inhaled. In a silence broken only by the crackling weed, we passed the joint between us. I felt the world outside gradually recede away to nothing, as I concentrated on her face, her fingers and the smoke swirling out of her lips.

When the tiny stub burned my fingers, I tossed it on to the floor, placed my arm around Liz's neck and kissed her deeply on the mouth. I could taste every crease in her lips, every twitch of her tongue. The difference between the hardness of her teeth and the softness of her mouth struck me as a miracle of evolution. For a while, our kiss became the entire universe.

Then she was taking off my shirt, and I was taking off her shirt, and it occurred to us that we really weren't getting very far like that, and we leaped off the bed, stripped ourselves and hopped back in.

84

Through a haze of mounting lust, I noticed that she kept her knickers on.

As we swamped each other in more kisses, I started trying to discreetly remove her pants without her noticing. In response, what had previously been an 'Mmmm' started turning itself into a 'Nnnn'. I had to try and hurry before the 'o' came along. My attempt to yank the pants over her buttocks made an ominous ripping sound and broke the spell.

'No,' she said. 'No sex.'

'Why?'

She kissed me, even more passionately than before.

'No sex,' she repeated, pausing to wipe saliva from her chin.

'Why?' I said, during the next pause for breath.

She answered me by turning me over on to my back and disappearing under the sheet.

'I love James,' she said, then shut me up by wrapping her mouth around the end of my penis.

For the rest of the week we hardly left the Rainbow Lodge, and spent our days smoking, eating, chatting, going for the occasional wander and having almost-sex.

For the first time, I actually liked India. The vibes with Liz were on the mend, and all the hassles of travelling seemed much less intense and demoralizing now that we had found a calm little enclave where we could pass the days.

I also lost my aversion to Indian yoghurt when I was introduced to Bhang Lassi, which is a drink made out of milk, yoghurt and hash. The superb thing was, you could order it from the hotel staff, which came in very handy when you were feeling too stoned to roll another joint. I didn't really like the taste, but became fond of Bhang Lassi anyway, since the best way to relieve the boredom of constant dope-smoking is to drink it.

There were loads of other travellers hanging out at the hotel, and because everyone shared joints it was an extremely sociable place. You ended up talking to a whole range of people, and most of our evenings were spent in pleasant, semi-comatose card-games which were dominated by the passing of spliffs and the exchange of ideas about travelling. I was mainly into the cards and the drugs, while Liz took to all the philosophizing with depressing enthusiasm.

No one ever seemed to get tired of talking about Indiaahh. I didn't see what there was to theorize about, and how you could possibly set about trying to *explain* a country, but everyone, it seemed, had a theory. Liz, predictably enough, lapped it all up, and I could tell that my cynicism about the whole thing was beginning to get on her nerves.

One guy, called Jonah, had been travelling almost non-stop for seventeen years. He claimed it had been almost a decade since he last wore shoes, and warbled on indefinitely about how inhuman it was to lose contact with the soil. He also said that whenever he encountered a beggar, instead of giving them money, he gave them a hug.

For hours on end, he held court over the group with tales of disease, robbery, drug abuse and foot-rot. These stories were just overtures, however, to help him draw a crowd. And it was only when he had a proper audience that he would embark on his favourite topic: a Unifying Theory of India.

'India,' says Jonah, 'is at the same time the most beautiful and the most horrific country – and Indians are both the warmest and the most brutal people on earth.'

Although Jonah has barely warmed to his theme, Belle,

an American hippie dressed in military fatigues, jumps in. 'India,' she says, 'is a beautiful country, but let's face it, guys – it's ruined by the people. They're all obsessed with money. They always want something off you. All they can think about is selling and buying.'

'You haven't scratched below the surface, man,' says Ing, a Scandinavian who has the build of a famine victim, but always seems to be eating. (Intestinal worm, according to Liz.) 'Commerce is simply a modern, kind of, thin sheet of plastic that has been wrapped over the rich carpet of India's history. I mean, this country has been invaded so many times, but it has always survived with its own culture in place. Capitalism is just the invader of today, and when it is defeated like all the other armies, there will be left behind the same spiritual people who always have lived here.'

'It's very cheap,' says Brian from Nottingham. 'You can get cheap things.'

'But . . . what's your name again?' stutters Belle.

'Ing.'

'Ing?'

'Ing.'

'But Ing – capitalism isn't going to vanish like all the other invaders. This time, India's lost the fight. Its character is disappearing. Only a fool can say that India is still a spiritual country.'

'In England,' says Brian, 'a banana costs up to twenty pence, but here you can get a bunch of ten to fifteen bananas for as little as thirty pee. That's a huge saving.'

'Let us not forget,' says Burl (Belle's boyfriend), 'that India has never recovered from British colonization. It will be two or maybe three more generations before Indians can truly respect themselves again. By which time it might be too late.'

'I love it here,' says Jonah, 'but I hate it here.' He nods sagely.

'I,' says Ing, 'hate it here. But I love it here.' He nods even more sagely than Jonah, who gets a bit miffed and tries to up the sageness quotient in his nod. This doesn't work because the miffiness shows through, so Jonah withdraws from the battle of nods and rolls another joint.

At this point, Xavier embarks on his theory. 'India, lack manee a beeg countray, souffers a crush under eetz own weight. Lack a whale own ze beach, ze size of eetz own self-population, eez ze mourder weapon of involunaree suiceede.'

Everyone looks at him blankly.

'J'aime l'Inde. Mais je la deteste,' he says, emphatically.

Everyone nods sagely, trying to show they understand French.

'It's fascinating, isn't it?' whispers Liz in my ear, her face alight with stimulation.

'It's all bollocks if you ask me.'

'How can you say that?'

'Easily. It's all bollocks.'

'But . . . all these theories. People who've travelled all over the world and are willing to share their experiences with us. Do you realize how lucky we are?'

'We're lucky not to be like them, that's for sure.'

She touches my cheek, and looks longingly into my eyes.

'Please, Dave. For me – just for me – will you please try and leave behind all this Western cynicism? Please. This is our chance to expand our minds. We have to take it.'

I look back at her. She has that look of desperate sincerity in her eyes that people get when they need sedation. Unable to think of a way to wriggle out of it, I decide that the only courteous thing to do is to lie.

'OK. I'm sorry. I'll try.'

'You promise?'

'I'll try and be more Eastern about things.'

Fortunately, she doesn't notice that I'm being sarcastic.

The real India

After a week in Manali, disaster struck. Jeremy turned up.

'I thought I'd find you here,' he said, as he emerged at the end of the path.

'J!' shrieked Liz, leaping from her chair and rushing to give him a kiss.

'Hi, Dave,' he said, apparently oblivious to the fact that we were supposed to hate each other's guts.

'Mmm.'

'I see you're partaking of the local poison.'

'No. I'm smoking a joint.'

'J! You were so right about this hotel. It's amazing,' gushed Liz.

'This hotel *is* Manali, it's as simple as that,' he replied. 'Now where's some weed?'

Without even asking, Liz took the joint out of my hand and passed it to Jeremy. He placed it between two fingers just under the knuckle, curled his hand into a fist and sucked the smoke out from around the base of his thumb.

Next thing I know, he's teaching Liz how to do the same thing.

'You'll notice a lot of the locals smoke like this,' he's saying.

*

Two days later, Jeremy tried to organize a day-trip. He told everyone in the hotel that there was a holy cave inhabited by Sadhus half-way up a nearby mountain, and that anyone who wanted to go should meet on the veranda first thing the following morning.

I was initially against the idea, just because it came from Jeremy. However, it was such a long time since I'd done anything active that the prospect of a long walk actually felt quite inviting. Also, if I wanted to stay in favour with Liz, it was important to show a bit of enthusiasm for something vaguely Eastern. A cave's a cave if you ask me, but since it was supposedly a holy one it satisfied Liz's mind-expansion credentials, so taking part in the trip would score me a few Brownie points. I decided to join in.

By ten o'clock a reasonable crowd had gathered: Burl, Belle, Ing and Jonah had all turned up, along with a guy call Ranj who was, of all things, Indian.

Shortly after we had set off, I spotted Liz (who was at the front of the group with Jeremy) giving a hug to a beggar. The beggar looked suitably disgusted by this behaviour, so I attempted to compensate by giving him a few rupees. Even though I couldn't see Liz's facial expression, I got the impression that post-hug, she had a whole new walk. Her body language now said, 'Everybody look at me – I'm just so damn serene it hurts.'

A mile or so down the road, it emerged that Jonah knew of a short cut. This burst Jeremy's bubble, which put me in an excellent mood, and left Liz at the back of the group, in charge of consoling him. I ended up talking to Ranj for most of the walk.

Ranj, it turned out, was from Putney. Instead of wearing all the traveller gear (which by now even I had bought), he was dressed in Levi's and a tight, freshly laundered T-shirt which showed off his toned muscles. He also sported the first hairstyle I'd seen since arriving in Manali.

He told me that he'd been dragged over by his parents to meet the family, but it had all just got too much for him, so he'd run away to the hills. He said his family was really rich and had contacts everywhere who would be out looking for him, so I shouldn't tell anyone that I'd seen him.

'Fair enough,' I said.

'I swear, they'll find me. Wherever I am, they'll find me and drag me back.'

'Are you sure you're not being a bit paranoid? I mean, it's a big country.'

'You don't know how it works here. My family's got their fingers in everything. I just need to say my name, and a total stranger will know what family I belong to, and word will get back to them of where I am. I swear to God. And I'll be in such deep shit when they find me.'

'Why?'

'Because I ran away, for fuck's sake!'

'But couldn't you tell them you just wanted to go back-packing?'

'Backpacking! You think they'd let me go backpacking! Travelling around like some low-life, with dirty clothes on my back, sleeping in bug-infested hotels with stinking hippies. Never in a million years would they let me go off like this. And on my own! Jesus Christ! They'd think I'd gone mad.'

'But I thought everyone did it.'

'Yeah, I mean, loads of my mates back home have done it. But not me. I'm not allowed.'

'Why not?'

'Because I'm Indian. And this is no way to behave for a respectable Indian.'

'Travelling's respectable.'

'Pah! Travellers are the scum of the earth.'

'But we're rich. We're Western.'

'So?'

'So we can afford to buy expensive things.'

'And . . . ?'

'So people act like they respect us.'

'Exactly. They *act like* they respect you. But they don't. They think you're dirty and tight-fisted, but they suck up to you because they want your money. Remember that. No Indian in this country will ever become your friend. Whatever they say to you is a lie – they only want your money.'

'You can't say that. It's racist.'

'Of course it's racist. I hate Indians, man. They're fucking barbarians. All they're interested in is money, money, money. I've been pinned down by ten thousand cousins all day every day for the last month, and all they want to talk about is stereos and cars and whisky and property prices, and it's driven me up the fucking wall, man. That's why I had to get out. I'm not interested in all that shit. I'm not interested in my dad's poxy business, and I couldn't give two shits if all his crappy clothes fall apart ten seconds after they've left the warehouse. It's all crap. It's materialist crap.'

'But I thought India was supposed to be, like, a spiritual country and everything.'

'That's why I've come travelling. I want to find the real India. I'm searching for, kind of, my spiritual motherland.'

'Like Manali.'

'Exactly.'

'And the Rainbow Lodge.'

'Exactly. This is it, man. Holy caves and all that shit. This is the stuff.'

'You're right,' I said. 'This is amazing.'

We walked along in companionable silence for a while, admiring the view.

'It's funny,' I said.

'What?'

'You know how Manali just feels right.'

'Yeah.'

'How you travel through all the stress and the money-grubbing, then you arrive here and, like, instantly know that you've found the real India and everything.'

'Yeah.'

'I mean, it's odd, because in all the time I've been up here, you're the first Indian I've had a conversation with.'

'So?'

'I dunno – it's as if the best bits – the bits that feel most like India – are the places where you don't have to talk to any Indians.'

'Too fucking right, man. Too fucking right.'

I ended up trying to explain this theory to Liz in the evening, and she almost burned me at the stake as a heretic. I'd never seen her so angry. For the time being, Jeremy was the royal favourite, and I was an incontinent corgi.

Maybe the places were the shit bits

Ranj was the first person I'd met since arriving in India who I actually liked. We got on well from the start, and while Liz drifted off into Bullshit Land with Jeremy, I started spending most of my time with Ranj. I'd never really had any friends from South London before, and it was interesting, because they really do have a different outlook on life.

After a fortnight or so, even Manali got boring, and it was somehow decided that Liz, Jeremy, Ranj and I would all travel to Dharamsala together. Apparently this was where the Dalai Lama and loads of Tibetan monks hung out, so it was bound to be a cool place. If you were really lucky, you'd even spot Richard Gere.

Manali had become a kind of security blanket, and the thought of leaving it behind made all my old fears creep back to the surface. I felt, though, that travelling in a big group would act as a form of insulation, and given that we had to move on at some point, this seemed like the best way to do it. Also, Dharamsala was meant to be quite like Manali, so the trip would be a gentle reintroduction to the rigours of proper travel.

*

As it turned out, none of us really liked Dharamsala, largely because we all ate something our first night that made us ill. I spent most of the night crapping, and Jeremy ended up vomiting out of his window. I knew it had been a mistake to order paella, but the Woodstock restaurant looked reasonably hygienic, and it just seemed like a fun change at the time.

Jeremy also kept on complaining that the place had become commercialized since he was last there, and that the Tibetans were cashing in on what was originally a place for spiritual reflection. He was really complaining about the fact that his once unique embroidered day-pack was now hanging up for sale outside every shop on the high street.

Just to piss him off, I bought one for myself.

We decided to rest up for a few days, then make a move from the mountains down to Rajasthan.

In order to get there, we had to take a bus all the way back to Delhi, followed by a train westwards to Jaipur. The whole thing took ages and was generally hot, smelly, dirty and uncomfortable. Also, not long into the journey Ranj started getting on well with Jeremy, which pissed me off.

Whenever the train or bus stopped, instead of getting frustrated by how long everything took, Ranj and Jeremy just got out, strolled and chatted with whoever was around, bought whatever food or tea was available, and consumed as much of it as they could before the train/bus spoilt their fun by moving off again. As soon as I started copying this technique, I began to enjoy myself.

The secret was to think of travel in a completely new way. If you took it as a way of getting from A to B, you were done for. You ended up eating your toes with frustration. You had to think of a journey as a state of being. It was an activity in its own right – a social ritual revolving around nourishment and conversation, fleetingly interrupted by pauses for motion. Basically, each trip was a little party.

For the first time, I ended up chatting to Indians, and even though none of them spoke decent enough English to say anything very interesting, most of the time they were amazingly friendly and ended up paying for my tea. I didn't even want them to pay, but often they insisted. This was quite a confusing experience, since up until then I'd been working on the never-trust-an-Indian-they're-a-bunch-of-criminals-who-believe-it's-their-moral-right-to-rip-you-off-because-you're-too-rich-for-your-own-good-and-you-still-have-the-blood-of-Empire-on-your-hands-so-even-if-they're-being-friendly-watch-out-they-want-something theory. A cup of tea only set them back about two pence, but I couldn't see what they were getting out of paying. It wasn't as if they all wanted me to help sponsor visa applications. Unless it was part of a long-term plan to befriend me for unspecified future use. Whatever the reason, it was nice to be treated in such a hospitable way.

Everywhere else, crowds of Indians wanted me in their shop, restaurant, hotel or rickshaw – the only people who talked to me wanted my money – but on a train, I was in a hassle-free zone. People either left me alone or chatted to me because, apparently, they just wanted a chat. After I'd been bought several teas by people who subsequently vanished without even asking for my address, I began to suspect that this might actually be genuine friendliness. It was all very strange.

I had assumed that travelling was the crap bit you had to tolerate in order to get to the places you wanted to see, but it occurred to me that maybe the places were the shit bits that you had to tolerate in order to do the travelling.

This whole thing was getting interesting. I could feel my 'Nnnn' turning into an 'Mmmm'.

Jeremy knew of a maaahvellous hotel, and as soon as we got to Jaipur, he insisted that we all go and take a look. It turned out to be pretty nice, so we all dumped our bags, washed and spent the rest of the day lolling around.

Liz and I were alone together in our room, mid loll, when I asked her if she fancied Jeremy.

'Don't be stupid.'

'It's not stupid.'

'Of course I don't fancy him! He's got a beard.'

'You swear?'

'Anyway, what if I did?'

'What if you did what?'

'What if I did fancy him?'

'I don't know . . .'

'You haven't got the right to stop me fancying people, you know.'

'I just thought that with me and you . . .'

'Me and you what?'

'You know – now that we're . . .'

'We're what?'

'You know. Now that we're having a, kind of, sexual relationship.'

'We are *not* having a sexual relationship, Dave.'

'Aren't we?'

'Of course we're not. Look – we're going to have to stop doing anything, now. I simply can't get through to you, can I?'

'But . . . we've been . . .'

'I have told you again and again that I love James. How many times do we have to go over this for you to get the message into your thick skull? It's not going to happen.'

'But it already has been happening.'

'What we've been doing doesn't mean anything. I thought that was clear. You said it yourself – we're just friends, and it's just a bit of fun. But you keep running away with these insane fantasies that we're in love, or something. I mean, it's going to have to stop. As of now. It's obvious that you simply can't handle it.'

'I didn't say we were in love. I'm not in love. I just thought . . .'

'Look – it was your idea in the first place, and you seemed to think that it would work, and I told you it wouldn't, and now it just isn't.'

'It is. I only asked you if you fancy Jeremy. Just forget it. Forget I spoke. Let's go back to before.'

'But that's exactly the point. This is the thin end of the wedge. I'm not going to have you staking out ownership of my body.'

'I haven't staked out your body, for God's sake!'

'That's the implication of what you said, and it's clear from the way you're talking that you feel you have some kind of ownership over me.'

'What are you talking about?'

'Look – I'm a free agent, and I'm telling you that from now on, we're just friends.'

'Oh, fuck off!'

'Don't you say that to me.'

'We're *not* just friends.'

'We are.'

'We can't be,' I shouted, 'because for one thing, I don't even like you. For fuck's sake! I don't know how I . . . You're impossible! You're . . . you're . . . I just can't . . . I mean . . . I don't know where to start. Your arse. Everything comes out of . . . you just talk out of your . . . I just don't know what I can say, when everything just . . . I mean it's all just a load of . . . of . . . FUCKING HELL!'

All of a sudden I was alone in the room, on the bed, kind of, almost, crying.

I emerged an hour or so later to find Jeremy holding court over Liz and a gang of four year-offers from his old school. They were all reminiscing about how three years previously, Jeremy had been their house captain. And this lot didn't have beards. The whole bunch of them were Rupert Everett look-alikes. Call me paranoid, but I could tell from Liz's flushed face that she had an erection.

That evening, inevitably, was taken up with a school reunion hosted by Jeremy, hostessed by Liz, and spoilt by me. Ranj wisely went out on his own.

For almost a quarter of an hour, they went on and on about how much of a coincidence it was that they'd bumped into each other, until I couldn't take the tedium of it any more.

'Look – it's not a coincidence. This whole country might as well be an extension of the sixth-form common-room for people like you, and you all stay in the same hotels for God's sake, so why don't you shut up about coincidences and move on to your crappy India theories.'

'Steady on,' said Rupert 1. 'There's no call for that.'

'I don't care what you say,' said Rupert 2, 'I think it's a bloody huge coincidence. I mean, how many people are there in this country? Bloody millions. And there's only four of us. That's a bloody big coincidence.'

'But you all come to the same places and you all do the same things, don't you? And it won't be a coincidence when you all meet up in the House of Lords in forty years, either.'

'Oh, so I suppose it's a conspiracy is it?' said Rupert 3.

'You can ignore Mr Downwardly-Mobile over there,'

said Jeremy. 'He thinks he's working class despite the fact that he went to public school. He's a social abseiler.'

'I did *not* go to public school. I went to an Independent School on an assisted place.'

'Assisted place? Oh, so we're playing the coalminer's daughter now, are we?'

I wasn't in the mood for an argument. I put my head down and concentrated on my food – shifting it around the plate with my fork. I had no appetite, but didn't want Liz to see how bad I was feeling, so I took a small mouthful.

'He's got a point, you know,' said Rupert 4. 'About the coincidence.'

The table went silent again. Jeremy, Liz and Ruperts 1 to 3 gave him hard stares.

Rupert 4 went bright red. 'Sorry,' he said, then carried on eating.

'Guess where we've just come from,' said Rupert 1 to Jeremy.

'Pushkar.'

'Bloody hell,' said Rupert 2. 'How did you know?'

'Educated guess.'

'See?' I said.

'Where did you stay?' said Jeremy.

'Krishna Rest House, wasn't it?' said Rupert 1.

'So you didn't discover the Peacock Holiday Resort, then?'

'No,' said Rupert 4, still looking a little upset. 'Is that the best place?'

'It's marvellous. And it's got the most charming garden. The only trouble is, you get woken up by the cries of peacocks in the morning.'

Liz gasped with anticipated pleasure. 'Oh, God. That sounds amazing. Can we go there?' She faltered for a second, realizing that she had asked the wrong person, then turned to me and smiled, splattering me with fake goodwill. 'Shall we go there?'

I shrugged a yes.

'Is it cheap?' said Liz, turning back to Jeremy.

'What do you think? Have I ever taken you anywhere expensive?'

'No,' said Liz.

'The place is a bargain. It's as simple as that. And don't tell too many people about it, or the price will go up.'

'Peacocks! Waking you up in the morning! God – I can't wait.'

'We haven't seen Jaipur yet,' I said.

'We don't need to spend too long here,' said Liz. 'It's far too touristy.'

'What are you talking about? You haven't even left the hotel.'

'I know, but it's on all the bus tours. Fat, rich, middle-aged tourists come here in air-conditioned buses to see Delhi, Jaipur and Agra. Everyone knows that.'

'The Silver Triangle,' said Rupert 4.

'Golden Triangle, old chap,' said Rupert 3.

'Sorry,' said Rupert 4.

'She's right,' said Jeremy. 'Jaipur has its charms, but it really is ruined by all these people on . . . on . . . *two-week holidays*. . . who come here and really don't have the slightest interest in the country. They just want to see a few palaces, buy some cheap carpets, then they go home happy, feeling they've learned something about Asia. I can't stand the sight of them, myself. They ruin all the tourist sights for the real travellers.'

'W-w-why d-d-do you say that?' said Rupert 4, as combatively as he could manage.

'Because they're so rich,' said Jeremy. 'Their bus is a

kind of high-tech cocoon, and they climb down at the tourist spots without having the slightest idea about how much things are supposed to cost, then they walk around happily paying double for everything – which gives Westerners a terribly bad name, and makes everything infinitely harder for the real travellers who are trying to get things for local prices.'

'After all,' I said, 'one doesn't want to ask daddy for money *too* often.'

Jeremy gave me a stare.

'That's absolutely right,' said Rupert 1. 'I hate asking daddy for money. I find it jolly humiliating, and I can't wait until I'm old enough to . . . to take him out for supper or something. I mean, that would be a great feeling.'

'Bloody right,' said Rupert 2.

The following day I went to the Palace of the Winds with Ranj, and I hate to say it, but Jeremy was right about the tourists. I quite liked the building though, even if it didn't look as good as the photo in The Book.

Outside, I was surprised to see that Ranj gave some money to a beggar.

'How can you tell which are the real beggars?' I asked him.

'What?'

'How can you tell the real beggars from the organized beggars?'

'What the fuck is an organized beggar?'

'You know – one who preys on tourists.'

'You are the most paranoid person I've ever met. A beggar's a beggar. Someone without any money. Who lives on the street.'

'Oh.'

'Don't you give them any money?'

'Jeremy said you weren't supposed to. He said that Indians just ignore them.'

'What a lying, tight-fisted wanker.'

'So you always give them money?'

'Not always. Just – you know – like in England. If I've got a bit of change, and the mood strikes me, I give some of it away.'

'Is that what most people do?'

'I don't know. I'm not telepathic. There isn't a rule book for what you're supposed to do, you know.'

'I suppose not.'

I felt bad now. It was all Jeremy's fault.

There was a story doing the rounds in our hotel about how a young tiger had escaped from Jaipur zoo by simply walking out of its cage between the bars. It had then, apparently, gone on a killing spree in a nearby village. We all thought this was a hilarious and typically Indian story until that evening, when a French guy chipped in with a new version. He claimed to have heard that the tiger had killed a Western traveller. A few people didn't believe him, but it made the rest of us really scared.

Jaipur clearly wasn't safe, partly because of the tiger, but mainly because Liz was drooling over all the Ruperts, so I made a big shit-eating statement about Jeremy's perceptive analysis of the city, and how we should move on to Pushkar. Ranj was reluctant to leave Jaipur so soon, and I was briefly faced with the horrific prospect of travelling alone with Liz and Jeremy.

'What – you're going *already*?' he said.

'Yeah, it's too touristy.'

'But you haven't seen it yet.'

'We have. We've done the Palace of the Winds.'

'What about the rest of it? It's a whole city.'

'Well, you know. We're not into cities, really. We've decided they're too hectic. And too materialist.'

'Where are you going then?'

'Pushkar.'

'What's Pushkar?'

'You must have heard of Pushkar.'

'No. What's in Pushkar?'

'Oh, it's really mellow, apparently. There's this lake, and . . . er . . .'

'And what?'

'I don't know, really. It's just apparently really mellow. A bit like Manali, but with a lake instead of mountains.'

'Right, right. Sounds quite cool.'

'And you never know – if you hang around here too long, someone's bound to spot you. No one will find you in Pushkar. It's just a village.'

'Maybe you're right. It is a bit mad here.'

'And there's peacocks at the hotel.'

'So?'

'Dunno. It just sounds cool. Oh, come with us. It'll be a laugh.'

'I'll think about it.'

That evening, I got the hotel receptionist to ask him if he was *the* Ranj Pindar.

He came with us.

Was it amazing?

It was in Pushkar that things went badly wrong between Liz and me. We were sitting reading in the courtyard of the hotel one morning (I was on a Wilbur Smith, and Liz had recently ditched the *Bhagavad Gita* in favour of *Zen and the Art of Motorcycle Maintenance*), when she suddenly leaped out of her chair and shrieked.

'Oh my Gooouuuurrrrd!'

'What?' I said, but she ignored me, sprinted to the courtyard entrance, and grabbed a girl who was just arriving with her rucksack.

'Fee!' cried Liz.

The girl turned round and looked at Liz, blankly.

'Fee – is that you?'

'I'm Fiona, yes.'

'It's me – Liz.'

There was a long pause while the girl scrutinized Liz, then, realization dawning, she screamed, even louder than Liz had done, 'OH... MY... GOOUUUUAAAARRRD! LIZZY!'

'Fee!'

'Lizzles!'

'Fifi!'

'This is just ... Gouard! ... unbelievable! How have

you . . . I mean how long have you . . . ? Bloody hell! Where do we start?'

'We . . . have . . . got . . . sooooo much to talk about.'

They spent about ten minutes exchanging vowels, saying each other's names over and over again with increasingly bizarre abbreviations, and admiring each other's jewellery, before Liz got round to introducing me.

'This is David, my travelling companion,' she said.

Fee extended a hand and allowed me to wobble her clammy, limp fingers.

'Charming,' she said, 'and this is my girlfriend, Caroline.'

It turned out that Liz and Fiona were best friends from the Ealing Junior String Orchestra, and had only seen each other once since Liz moved house, aged eleven.

Fiona went upstairs with Caroline to 'freshen up', promising to come back down for a 'good old chin-wag' in a few 'minny moes.' She eventually re-emerged and glided down the stairs with the filth cleaned off her face, and her greasy hair freshly brushed and tied back. Oddly, this made her look even worse than before.

'It's soooo good to see you,' she oozed, squeezing Liz's hand.

'And *such* a coincidence.'

'Amazing.'

'Unbelievable.'

'I think Krishna must have wanted us to get together again,' said Fiona, 'otherwise it couldn't possibly have happened.'

'And . . . and . . . where have you just come from? How long have you been here?'

'Caz and I have just finished three months at a leper colony in Udaipur, actually.'

'WHAT!' I said, dropping my book on the floor.

'Yah. It was amazing.'

I moved my chair back a few extra inches, just in case.

'You've just spent three months in a leper colony!?'

'Well – I mean, they don't call them that any more – it's now known as the Udaipur Leprosy Rehabilitation Centre and Hospice – but it's the same thing.'

'Jesus fucking Christ! What d'you do that for?' I said.

'Oh, it's amazing.'

'Yeah, I've always wanted to do that,' said Liz.

'*What?*'

Liz gave me an evil look. 'I didn't bother mentioning it because I knew you wouldn't understand. It's always been a dream of mine, actually.' She turned back to Fiona and sweetened up her face again. 'Fee, darling, what was it *really* like? Was it amazing?'

'Oh, absolutely. I'm a changed person.'

'Of course.'

'How?' I said.

'Just – my karma is completely different.'

I didn't even want to know what that meant.

'God, it sounds amazing,' said Liz.

'I mean, I've learned so much about myself . . . about healing . . . and stuff.'

'How did you get a place there? I mean I've heard it's quite competitive.'

'I was lucky. One of mother's friends runs a leprosy organization in London, and I was put to the head of the queue. I could put in a good word for you if you like.'

'Oh, would you? That would be brilliant. I mean, I'm *definitely* coming here again, and next time I'd like to give something back to India in return for what it's given me.'

'Exactly. That's why *I* wanted to do it. I mean I hadn't been here before, but I knew this is what it would be like, and with my contacts in leprosy, it seemed like too good an opportunity to miss.'

'But . . . isn't it dangerous?' I asked.

'Don't be silly. Leprosy is an entirely curable disease if you catch it at the early stages. And it's not nearly as infectious as people think.'

'But . . . it's disgusting.'

'You have to get over that. My first few days were awful, but now I feel more at home amongst lepers than I do with the able-bodied.'

'But . . . did you cure people?'

'No – our place was for people once they've reached the incurable stage. That's what makes Udaipur so popular.'

'Why?'

'Because it's fascinating. You get worse cripples there than anywhere else, and you have to wash them and assist their walking, and generally try and help them to live with their disease.'

'*Wash* them?'

'Yes – I got rather addicted to that.'

'WHAT?'

'It's horrible at first, but once you get used to it, it's an amazing feeling.'

'Why?'

'Because once you've done it, you feel so . . . *good*.'

'How?'

'You just feel like a *good* person. You feel like you've earned positive karma. You feel as if you've cleansed away all the horrible privileges that you were born with, and you're stripped down to just a simple girl, scrubbing the back of a filthy, scabby, dying leper. It's absolutely exhilarating.'

'Oh, I must do it,' said Liz. 'I really must.'

'But isn't it, like, depressing?'

'Oh no! Quite the opposite. The place is awash with optimism.'

'But I thought you said they were all incurable.'

'They are, but they're all so charming. I mean, they've got nothing left, and they've usually been rejected by their families, and they're about to die, but they can all still laugh and be positive about life.'

'Yeah, right.'

'It's true.'

'That's not possible.'

'It's true. You see, there's an interview policy. The hospice is massively oversubscribed, and to get a bed there you have to pass an interview to prove that you've got the right attitude.'

'Which is what?'

'Positive. You have to be positive. I mean, if they were just sulking all the time, the girls who went would be miserable and wouldn't learn anything.'

'Are you saying that the patients are selected to suit the nurses?'

'All hospitals are like that. I mean, if you don't have the right disease, you can't get in. If you aren't ill enough, you can't get in. This is just taking it one step further. And I tell you, they get better treatment there than they would for miles around. That's why the atmosphere is so good. It's simply a marvellous place.'

'That's sick.'

'What – you think it would be better if they didn't get any treatment at all?'

'No, but I mean, selecting patients like that . . .'

'You have to be selective. I mean, there are lepers growing on trees in this country.'

'Yes, but . . .'

'Actually, between you and me, the government education programme is beginning to have an effect, and the supply's been drying up a bit lately.'

At that point, Caroline joined us.

'Hi-eey,' she sung.

'Hi-eey,' sung Fiona in return. 'Feeling better?'

'A bit.'

'Did you just do another one?'

'Another three.'

'Oh God. It's getting worse, isn't it?'

'Mmm.'

'Don't you think it might be time to try a doctor?'

'I thought we agreed that we don't believe in doctors.'

'Maybe we can find a homeopathic one.'

'If you think so . . .'

'Are you ill?' said Liz, radiating concern.

'Yeah, I can't stop going to the loo, and I've lost a stone and a half.'

'You've lost a stone and a half?' said Liz.

'Yeah.'

'Oh, you lucky thing.'

'I know, but I'm beginning to get a bit worried now because I keep on fainting.'

'How come you don't believe in doctors when you've just been working in a hospital?' I said.

'It wasn't a hospital, it was a hospice,' said Fiona. 'And it had healers instead of doctors.'

'What's the difference?'

'Doctors cure the disease. Healers heal the person.'

'Who do you go to for the shits?'

Liz gave me a despairing look.

The from-a-height thing

The arrival of Fee and Caz heralded the beginning of the end. Liz started getting up every morning before breakfast to go and meditate by the lake with them, and under their influence, she started turning into a cross between Princess Anne, Mother Teresa, Gandhi and Russell Grant.

Meanwhile, Ranj seemed to be going off the rails. It all began to go wrong when he bought a chillum, which is basically a cross between a pipe and a traffic cone, designed for smoking vast quantities of hash. One chillum could probably keep the entire population of Barnet stoned for a week. Ranj, however, acquired the unusual habit of smoking an entire chillum on his own. For breakfast. Then another one for lunch.

Normally, it was impossible to get more than two puffs into a joint before some unknown scrounger would come and sit next to you and start a feeble attempt at a conversation in anticipation of a few drags. Ranj's chillum, however, was so fearsome that it actually frightened people away. A busy courtyard of travellers could be almost cleared by the sight of a strangely boggle-eyed Indian sucking on one end of what looked like an industrial cooling tower having a bad day. The smoke it produced often appeared to be heavier than air, and most of the time Ranj sat contentedly in a puddle of fumes, rolling his eyes, swearing at imaginary members of his family and occasionally passing out.

Now I'm all in favour of drug abuse, but by this stage Ranj just wasn't good company any more. He wasn't company at all. As a result, most of my time in Pushkar was spent alone with Wilbur Smith.

Jeremy, meanwhile, had been ousted from the royal entourage by Fee and Caz. He didn't seem to mind too much, though, and I almost thought I detected a certain relief that he was now being left alone by Liz. Whenever I saw him he was alone in the courtyard, reading a book called *The Teachings of Don Juan: A Yaqui Way of Knowledge* by Carlos Castaneda.

Feeling briefly sympathetic towards him as a fellow cast-off, I asked him what it was about.

'It's a must-read,' he said, in that pompous voice I'd almost forgotten.

Bye-bye sympathy.

'Here – read the back,' he said.

'"*Don Juan* projects a quality of experience beside which scientific exactitude stands in peril of paling into insignificance. – Theodore Roszak,"' it said.

'Blimey. Sounds good.'

'I'll swap it for your Wilbur Smith when you've finished,' he said.

'All right.'

One morning, I was tucking into a banana pancake when Liz, Fee and Caz, just back from their dawn seance or whatever it was they did, came and joined me for breakfast (one boiled egg each, in case you're interested).

Despite the fact that I would far rather have been left alone with Wilbur, they seemed to think that the courteous thing to do was to come and sit at my table, disturb my peace and talk unadulterated shit to each other without addressing a word to me.

I tried to blot them out and concentrate on the bananariness of my pancake, but the invasion was just too brutal.

'Did you get there today?' said Fee.

'What – to nirvana? Are you crazy?' said Liz.

'No – not nirvana. To the other one. The one below nirvana but above tranquillity that I was telling you about. What's it called again?'

'Thingummy,' said Caz.

'That's the one.'

'I definitely got to tranquillity,' said Liz.

'Brilliant,' said Fee. 'I mean, that's the basis. You're well on the way now.'

'I think it's the first time I properly got there, actually.'

'Oh, I'm so happy for you. How did it feel?'

'It felt . . . um . . . kind of . . .'

'Tranquil?' I offered.

No response.

'. . . as if . . . as if my body belonged to someone else, and I was just a guest in my own head, observing the world and myself from a height.'

'That's amazing,' said Caz. 'That's more than tranquillity. I think that's the next one up. I hardly ever get the from-a-height thing.'

'Really?'

'Yeah. You're doing really well.'

Liz sighed.

'I am soooo glad I bumped into you two,' she said, touching each of them on the leg. 'You've opened my eyes to . . . to . . . to the WORLD!'

Oh Christ, I thought. She really has lost it now.

'My karma,' she went on, 'really has changed. I'm into a whole new realm.'

I couldn't take this any more.

'Karma?' I said, slowly. 'Karma? My fucking arse. Why don't the three of you get a life?'

Silence descended on the table. Fee and Caz stared at me, their facial expressions utterly in tune with one another. Neither of them looked even the slightest bit angry with me, or even offended. They both, quite transparently, just felt sorry for me. In their eyes, I was now on a par with the lepers.

Liz, however, didn't feel sorry for me. This much was obvious. I was on the receiving end of one of her looks. Not, in fact, *one* of her looks, but *the* look. This was a *serious* look. Translated into English it said, basically, 'That's it.' I had reached the end of the road. She'd had enough of me.

'Come on, Fee. Come on, Caz,' she said.

They took their boiled eggs and moved to another table.

That afternoon, in a complex operation of ostentatious secrecy, Liz moved her mattress and backpack into Fee and Caz's room.

That's that, then

Dear Mum & Dad, –
Sorry it's been such a long time since I wrote to you, but I've been
having an amazingly busy time. I have now left the Himalayas and am
in Pushkar – a beautiful and peaceful lakeside village buried in the
deserts of Rajasthan – probably the most colourful state in India,
famous for the brightly coloured saris worn by the women, and for
the equally lurid spices on sale in its crowded markets. I've been
having a very relaxing time here, even though things with Liz haven't
been going very well lately. We seem to hate each other's guts at
the moment, but I'm sure things will pick up soon.
                    lots of love,
                        Dave

I was sipping my afternoon tea – one of many afternoon
teas – in the hotel courtyard a few days after Liz's defection,
when I heard the sound of screeching tyres coming from
immediately outside. There didn't seem to be many cars in
India, and hardly any in Pushkar – let alone ones that could
get up enough speed to be able to screech to a halt – so I
looked up from my book to see what was going on.

A fat man with a moustache, dressed in jacket and tie,
appeared in the courtyard at a run, looking stressed. He
examined us all one by one, then, when he saw the blob in
the corner that used to be Ranj, he started howling.

The howl brought three more people into the court-yard, one of whom was a woman in a sari. She took one look at Ranj, then screamed and fainted. The other two people were youngish guys in jeans and designer T-shirts.

'Fuckin'ell man,' said one of them. 'You fuckin' twat.' I recognized the language as deepest Putney. This was obviously a brother. He grabbed Ranj by the arms, but Ranj refused to support his own weight, so the second young guy approached and took him by the other arm. Together, they frogmarched him out of the courtyard.

Ranj didn't particularly seem to wake up through the whole episode until I heard his voice wafting in from outside, saying 'Wait . . . Wait . . . Wait . . . WAIT! JUST WAIT.'

Ranj then reappeared, on doddery legs, and walked up to me.

'I want you to have this,' he said, putting his chillum into my hand, and closing my fingers around it.

'Thanks, man,' I said.

He gave me one last don't-mind-me-I'm-just-off-to-the-gallows look and tottered away, into the arms of a waiting brother.

The pair of them disappeared, and the car's engine started up. It then cut out, and I heard the sound of a car door slamming and an argument. All I could make out was someone saying, 'He's not worth it. He's not worth it.'

There was a lull for a second, then the bigger of the two brothers appeared in the courtyard, marched up to me, grabbed me by the shirt, pulled me out of my chair, and slammed me against the wall.

'Are you his dealer, then?' he shouted. 'ARE YOU? DID YOU DO THIS TO HIM?'

'No, man. I've never dealt in my life,' I stammered, suddenly convinced that I was about to be killed.

'DID YOU SELL THAT SHIT TO HIM? DID YOU?'

'I d-d-didn't. I s-swear to God.'

'I SHOULD FUCKIN' KILL YOU!'

'You've got the wrong person. I swear on my life. On my mother's life.'

He let go of me, and snarled.

'Scum. You fucking scum.'

Then he spat on my shoes, and left.

The hotel receptionist shouted something at him in Hindi, and in response he tossed a few banknotes on to the ground as he disappeared around the corner.

I rearranged my shirt and tried to get my breath back. The entire courtyard was silent, and everyone was staring at me. I tried to chuckle and say that the guy was a loony, but no sound would come out of my mouth.

I then noticed that Liz, Fee and Caz had watched the whole thing from a balcony above. Liz, I could tell, was almost wetting herself with delight, but was straining every facial muscle to keep her pleasure hidden behind the smug, disappointed, told-you-so look that was plastered over her features.

Fee and Caz, judging by appearances, just felt sorry for me.

I had barely recovered from my brush with death when Liz descended from the temple that was Fee and Caz's room to give me 'some news'.

'What? What is it?' I said, still feeling a little rattled.

'I've made a decision. There's something I have to do.'

'What?'

'Well – Fee and Caz have been telling me about a place, not far from here, that I'd like to visit.'

'So?'

'It's not the kind of place that you can just go and look at, though. If you want to go there, you have to make a commitment to stay at least two weeks.'

'What! Why?'

'It's an ashram.'

'An ashram? What's an ashram when it's at home?'

'It's a Hindu place of retreat for meditation, reflection and spiritual furtherance.'

'*Spiritual furtherance*? What are you talking about?'

'Look – I don't want to go over this ground with you again. You're obviously impervious to ... to what this country is trying to teach you, and I think we should just stick with the facts. I am going to go to the ashram with Fee and Caz.'

'For two weeks?'

'For at least two weeks.'

'Well that's that, then.'

'What's what?'

'You've abandoned me. That's it. I'm on my own.'

'No, you're not. I realize you don't want to come to the ashram with us, but we can always meet up ...'

'Too sodding right I'm not coming to an ashram. I don't want to get brainwashed by some bunch of Hare Krishna loony mental headcases. No way. I'm not going anywhere near ...'

'Stop. STOP! I don't want to hear this. Your prejudices are ...'

'PREJUDICES! I'm not prejudiced – I just don't want to end up running around Leicester Square with a shaved head telling everyone I love them.'

'That, Dave, is called prejudice, in case you didn't know

what the word means. We're talking about a whole religion here, followed by hundreds of millions of people, and all you can think of is some ... some ... typically twisted Western manifestation of an Eastern philosophy. You are *so* closed-minded, I really don't know why you even bothered coming here.'

'Because you persuaded me to.'

'Don't give me that. You wanted to come.'

'Only so I could be with you. And now you're deserting me.'

'I'm following a calling. You're welcome to join me, or to meet me afterwards, but I am not going to sacrifice this opportunity just for the sake of your petty-mindedness.'

'And I'm not just going to hang around waiting for you. We've got an itinerary to keep up with. There's a whole country out there that I came here to see. I can't just waste all my time here, can I? I'd go mad. There's no point in coming to India and not seeing anything. I've got to get moving. I have to get to Goa.'

'Impatience is a typically Western state of mind. You don't realize it, but you've become a self-parody.'

'*I've* become a self-parody? That's hilarious!'

'What do you mean by that?'

'You ... you ... you've just become an arsehole. That's the only way of putting it. And you haven't even got enough personality to become a self-parody. You've become a parody of someone else. Despite the fact that Fiona is one of the biggest bullshitters ever to walk this earth, you have decided to try and turn yourself into her! It's pathetic.'

'If you had said that to me a week ago, I would have got angry. Fortunately for you, in the last few days I have made significant progress, and have come to know myself well enough for a pathetic little shit like you to be unable to get to me. My real self is simply impervious to the likes of you.

Whatever you say, you simply can't offend me, you ... you slimy little PIECE OF SHIT! YOU TURD! YOU FEEBLE MOANING CYNICAL PATHETIC PSEUDO-LAD PISS-HOLE FAKE! I HATE YOU AND I NEVER WANT TO SEE YOU AGAIN YOU FUCKING ARSEHOLE! YOU MAKE ME SICK!'

Cross-cultural interchange

And so it was that I ended up on my own. Ranj had been kidnapped by his family, Liz had become a Hare Krishna, and Jeremy was just a lost cause as a human being. Other than them, there was no one I knew in the entire country.

By this stage I was bored of Pushkar. After the argument with Liz I felt that I ought to get moving in order to give the impression that I wasn't frightened of being alone, but the fact was, even the *thought* of travelling on my own made my already loose bowels take on the character of a deflating balloon.

I did not want to be on my own. I just didn't. There was only one thing in the world that would have been worse than being alone, and that was being with Jeremy.

Pushkar was such a small place that it didn't even have a railway station. The nearest one was a few hours away by bus, in Ajmer. As I walked alone to the Pushkar bus station to buy myself a ticket to Ajmer, I felt like one of those old men who amble around in parks feeding ducks, eating sandwiches out of a paper bag and trying to talk to strangers. This was bleak. Nineteen years old, and I already felt like a lonely pensioner.

I couldn't recall ever having felt lonely before. It was a

weird sensation – for the moment a bit exciting, but I could tell that once I got used to it, it would be awful.

Our plan had been to stop in Udaipur, Ahmedabad and Bombay before we got to Goa, but I decided to ditch the original itinerary and head straight there. This meant that I would be going half-way down the entire country in one go, but I couldn't face stopping in places where I might end up in some hotel on my own, without any other travellers. I mean, there'd be *some* people in each of those places, but I'd already learned that in big towns, travellers weren't very friendly. And I didn't even really want to see Udaipur, Ahmedabad and Bombay, anyway. I mean, a city's a city.

If I could just grit my teeth and make it on my own to Goa, I'd be able to hang out there and meet some new people. I was bound to find someone who'd travel with me. Maybe even a female. A lot of that kind of thing went on in Goa, apparently.

I turned to the map of India at the front of The Book and worked out from the scale that the width of my little finger corresponded to roughly two hundred miles. I then measured Pushkar to Goa, and it came out at six little-finger-widths. That couldn't be right. One thousand two hundred miles? I didn't even know the whole country was that length.

Whatever. I closed the book. This was clearly a long journey. But it would be worth it in the end. After all, I still had precisely two hundred condoms left. (Fortunately, the condoms were in my rucksack, and whatever happened when we finally separated, I was going to make damn sure that I took *all* of them with me.)

With a ticket to Ajmer in my money belt, I spent the rest of the day phrasing my farewell speech to Liz, and finally settled on:

'I realize that things have been difficult, and that whatever happens we'll never be able to say that we parted on the friendliest of terms – but I just want you to know that I forgive you for what you've done to me, and I won't hold it against you that you abandoned me. I wish you all the best on your spiritual journey, and I thank you for giving me the opportunity to travel alone in Asia.'

Unfortunately, when I woke up the following morning, she had already left. I found a note on the floor of the room which said,

D,

Bye.

Peace,

L.

I crumpled up the note angrily, then decided that I wanted to keep it and flattened it out on the floor, folded it up and slipped it into The Book.

With a start, I realized that I had overslept and was late for my bus. Liz had normally taken charge of the getting-up-in-time-to-catch-buses side of things. Shit. In fact, she had taken charge of everything.

I got dressed, threw the stray piles of scattered clothes into my pack, put my shoes on, checked under the bed, then paused for a second, threw my stuff out on to the bed and counted the condom boxes. Yup. Thought so. There were two missing.

Some fucking ashram *she* was visiting. Typical. So that's what she meant by spiritual furtherance. Absolutely typical.

I contemplated the pile of condom boxes on the bed, all

of them with the Cellophane still intact, and felt briefly paralysed. I was a failure. My life was a mess. I belonged in a monastery.

However miserable I felt, it dawned on me that missing my bus wasn't going to improve the situation, so I forced myself to repack my bag and head for the bus station. I arrived almost a quarter of an hour late, but fortunately the bus was still there. To my horror, though, I saw that the front three seats of the bus were already occupied by Liz, Fee and Caz.

My seat was in the row directly behind them, and as I got on, Fee and Caz smiled at me in the way you'd smile at a naughty leper. Liz looked the other way.

Despite the fact that it was only a short journey, Caz managed to puke out of the window twice. Due to the speed of the bus, a significant portion of vomit flew out of her window and back in through mine, splattering me in the face.

How apt, I thought, as I wiped half-digested flakes of lentil from my face. First you steal my travelling partner, then you puke in my face. Do you have any other desires? Would you like to crap in my bed?

Ajmer isn't the kind of place where you'd actually want to stay, and given that Fee, Liz and Caz were on the same bus as me to Ajmer, it seemed a fair bet they'd be heading on somewhere else by train. We didn't speak on the bus, not even, for example, to apologize for vomit shrapnel, so the details of their onward journey remained a mystery.

The bus stand in Ajmer turned out to be small and almost empty of buses. This made it pretty clear that they were going to be continuing their journey by rail. The bus station was on the opposite side of town to the railway station, and having seen the three of them squeeze into a rickshaw with their rucksacks, I got a separate rickshaw on my own and followed them across town.

I lost sight of them during the journey, only to find them again at the railway station, right in front of me in the queue for trains heading south to Udaipur. None of them turned round to look at me, but I could tell that my presence had been registered by the way they all stiffened up and started exchanging fevered whispers.

After about ten minutes, Liz spun round, bright red with anger.

'Are you following us?'

'No.'

'Just tell me why you're doing this, Dave. Precisely what do you think you're getting out of this?'

'Nothing. I'm just travelling south, and this is the way.'

'Is it some twisted form of revenge?'

'I don't know what you're talking about. Where else am I going to go? Back up to Delhi?'

'Very funny.'

'It wasn't a joke.'

'You're not going to intimidate us, you know.'

'I'm not trying to intimidate you, for God's sake. I'm just making my way to . . . to . . . Udaipur and Ahmedabad.'

She eyed me suspiciously.

'I thought you said you were going to Goa.'

'Yeah, well I'm stopping on the way, aren't I? I'm not just interested in travellers' hang-outs you know. I want to see the real India.'

She eyed me even more suspiciously.

'We're getting off before Udaipur – I'm not telling you where – but if you get off at the same station as us, I'm calling the police.'

'Yeah, right.'

'I'm not joking.'

'And what are they going to do?'

'That depends on what I tell them you've done.'

'Oh, Liz. Give me a break.'

'No – you give me a break.'

'Look – I don't know what we're arguing about, because I haven't got the slightest interest in following you off the train and going to your sordid little brainwashing centre. I am going, like I said, to Udaipur.'

'I'm not interested in your lies any more, David. Just remember, I'm calling the police if this carries on any longer.'

When I got to the front of the queue, I tried to explain to the ticket-seller that I wanted to be in a different compartment to the three English girls. It took ages for him to get what I was on about, but eventually he sighed, nodded and told me that he understood.

I paid for the ticket, and he passed it under the glass with a huge wink, saying that he'd put me as close as possible.

On the train, I was greeted with more frosty glances and rigid turned backs. I felt as if I'd already finished with the lonely-pensioner phase and was now a dirty old man in a mac.

After a while, the man sitting next to me smiled and said, 'These girls your friend?'

He was wearing a green polyester shirt, blotched with sweat, and looked as if he had recently washed his hair in lard. We were wedged up against one another on the seat, but whenever I tried to create a little space between us, his fat oozed outwards to fill the gap.

'No. Not my friends,' I replied.

'You go talk with girls, yes?'

'No. No talk with girls.'

'Why?'

'They no my friend.'

The man looked at me as if I was certifiably insane, partly because I had slipped into a pidgin English even worse than his, but mainly, I suppose, because I showed no interest in talking to the girls.

'They no good girls,' I said, hoping to explain myself.

'They beautiful girls,' he replied with a huge, goggle-eyed leer.

'Believe me, they are pains in the arse beyond belief.'

'Hello, what?'

'Bad girls. Bad girls.'

'Bad girls fun.'

'No. Not these ones. No bloody fun whatsoever.'

He wobbled his head in sympathy, obviously still thinking that I was insane.

'What is your good name?' he said.

'Dave.'

'Where are you from?'

'England.'

'Ahh. England very good. Are you married?'

'No.'

'What is your job?'

'Student.'

'Ah, very good.'

At this point, we ran out of steam. There was a long silence. I realized I ought to have asked the same questions back, but I somehow didn't have the energy. The silence was broken when the man sitting opposite me, who looked so ill I didn't want to touch him, leaned forward and tried to shake my hand.

'Hello,' I said, with a little wave.

'Good day, sir,' he replied, shaking my leg. 'What is your good name?'

'Dave.'

'Where are you from?'

'England.'

'Ahh. England very good. What is your job?'

'Student.'

'Are you married?'

'No.'

'Ah, very good.'

I was really meeting the locals now. Talk about cross-cultural interchange – this was fascinating.

A few hours later, when Liz, Fee and Caz left the train, I pretended not to notice. They tried to do it slowly and unobtrusively, but I saw that the second they hit the platform, they sprinted off through the station, then out of sight.

Now I really was alone.

The lard-hair man clicked his tongue against the roof of his mouth, nodded upwards, flicked the fingers of his right hand outwards and said, 'Beautiful girls.'

Somehow, I understood what he meant. In the international language of greasy sex-starved men, those gestures said, 'Unlucky, mate – they were out of our league anyway.'

I clicked my tongue, nodded upwards and shrugged.

He laughed and patted me on the knee.

It was slightly depressing to realize that I spoke Greasy Sex-Starved Man so fluently.

And I'm not from Surrey

The train terminated in Udaipur, and I was one of the last people to leave the compartment. Stepping out on to the dark platform, I saw that the station was almost deserted. Almost deserted by Indian standards, that is – which means that there are so few people around, you can occasionally discern the odd inch of floor visible beneath the swirling heaps of humanity.

From the station forecourt, I took a look at the cabs and rickshaws. Despite the hour of the day, the city looked busy. Because of my final conversation with Liz, I felt as if I ought to visit slightly more than just the railway station.

A driver came up to me and tried to drag me to his rickshaw, but I reacted so angrily he retreated. This made me realize, fleetingly, that Jeremy had been right about how you learn to be so brutal with people that they leave you alone. And you don't even notice yourself changing – it just suddenly dawns on you that you're getting hassled much less.

This thought provided me with a few tenths of a second of happiness, before I began to feel depressed again. I knew it was important not to let myself get into a downward spiral, so I decided to allow myself a little indulgence. I wasn't going to bother with Udaipur. I was going to take a 'Retiring Room' in the station (there are hotel-type rooms in most big Indian stations), and would get a train the next morning, further south to Ahmedabad.

I turned back inside and joined the queue at a ticket kiosk.

All the second-class seats were taken for the train to Ahmedabad, so as part of my emotional-welfare campaign I decided to splash out on a first-class ticket. This cost four entire days' worth of budget, but at least it made me feel better.

This time the sensation of well-being lasted several whole seconds, before depression rushed in again.

My Retiring Room, I discovered, was clean and well-ordered, which somehow depressed me just as much as if it had been dirty. The precision of the room and the emptiness of the bed next to me, the pattern on the floor, the hole in the mesh over the window, the shape of my rucksack – suddenly everything I looked at seemed to contribute to making me feel worse.

I decided to try and cheer myself up by writing a postcard home. I found a crumpled picture of Manali at the bottom of my pack and sat myself at a rickety writing-table in the corner of the room.

Dear Mum & Dad,
Udaipur is a fascinating and colourful city in the southern part of Rajasthan. I've just arrived here, and am hoping to visit the Lake Palace Hotel tomorrow, where a bit from one of the James Bond films was filmed. Liz has ditched me and run off with two Sloanes, so I'm now all on my own and am feeling severely depressed. My stomach also feels a bit weird, so I think I'm probably about to get ill, which isn't very good timing, because there's no one to look after me now. Don't worry, though. I'm sure things will be fine soon.
                                        love,
                                        Dave
PS How are things at home?

I perched the card on top of my backpack, put the light out and went to bed. The sheets seemed relatively clean, but I was in the kind of mood where it's impossible to forget how many people have slept in the same bed, and the variety of acts that have been enjoyed on the same absorbent mattress. I began to feel itchy and needed something to take my mind off things.

Having switched the light back on, I opened my book and managed to take some comfort from the fact that the main character was obviously having a worse time than me (puking his guts out in the Mexican desert and running around naked thinking he was a dog). I couldn't concentrate for more than one sentence at a time, though, and ended up just listening to the trains outside my window.

I switched off the light and tried to fall asleep, but was distracted by visions of Liz which kept on popping into my head. I couldn't stop myself from seeing her sitting around with Fee and Caz, having a laugh, meditating, and bitching about me. I was determined not to dream about how the three of them would have endless fun while I withered away in lonely hotel rooms on my own, and I tried to make myself think about something else. The subject which kept on rushing in to fill the void, however, was even worse, with my brain insisting on doing mental calculations of how many days I'd done, and how many days I had left in India. It seemed of crucial importance to work out whether or not I was more than half-way through, but I didn't really want to think about that either, because there was definitely still a long time left, and it seemed likely that I was going to find myself unable to enjoy any of it.

The only way to stop my mind swirling with awful thoughts was to try and empty it altogether. This proved almost impossible, with images of Liz, Fee, Caz, Jeremy, my mum and bizarre Asian sex acts in Udaipur Railway

Retiring Rooms perpetually filling my brain. I thought back, straining to remember if I had eavesdropped any tips on meditation from the three girls, but nothing useful came to mind.

I ended up just repeating 'void void void' over and over again in my head, so obsessively that it blotted out any other word, and concentrating all my remaining powers on trying to visualize an empty box. I kept on getting distracted by the feeling that it might actually be working, but eventually deduced that I must have fallen asleep from the fact that I was waking up and it was light.

With the new day, I found myself feeling marginally happier and took breakfast in the station restaurant. There *was* something a bit cool about being on your own. If nothing else, I felt brave, and that at least was a positive feeling. Watching all the other people eating in groups, I decided that I must look slightly mysterious. That also felt good. I'd never really felt mysterious before. And, to cap it all, my omelette genuinely tasted nice. Yes – this was a good day. Yesterday had been a bad day, but this, I decided, was going to be a good day.

It wasn't. My compartment from Udaipur to Ahmedabad was shared with a kid who screamed incessantly, a girl who ate incessantly, a boy who hit the kid who screamed incessantly, their mother who hit the kid for complaining he was being hit by his brother, and her husband, who looked as if he wanted to kill himself. They were so noisy and took up so much space that I spent the entire eleven hours feeling like an unwanted social worker in a psychotic family's living room.

Ahmedabad station stank of shit – literally – and I had to reach new pinnacles of threatening and lying behaviour before succeeding in buying my onward ticket, eventually using the pretext that my wife was about to give birth in a Bombay hospital.

This train finally set off long after dark. I was feeling fragile, so as soon as the train had started moving, I climbed up to my top bunk and tried to forget where I was. I usually left my rucksack under the lowest bed, but with no one around I trusted, the only way to make sure that nothing could get stolen was to use it as a pillow. This made my feet stick out from the bottom of the bed, and I ended up kicking most of the people walking up and down the carriage in the head. Some of them got a bit stroppy about this and tried to get me to move my bag, but I pretended to be either stupid or asleep, or both.

As I dozed off, I vaguely remembered someone telling me that you should always sit cross-legged because it's a dire insult to show the soles of your feet to a Hindu. I thought this might have something to do with them being reluctant to have sweaty socks wiped on their forehead, so I made a token attempt to curl up. After all, it would be pretty stupid to get lynched purely because you were trying to avoid getting robbed.

I woke at dawn and did a quick scout of the train for other travellers, but couldn't find anyone. I was in no mood to try and talk to Indians and spent most of the morning hiding up in my bunk feeling lonely and depressed.

Around lunch-time, the train pulled to a stop in the middle of nowhere, and after a while people started getting out. I hopped down from my bed and followed the crowd out of the door. We were high on an embankment above a swamp, with one other track next to us. I had assumed that people were leaving the train to try and find out what was happening, but it turned out that everyone was contentedly stretching their legs, smoking, chatting or pissing. I wandered around for a while, and a few people smiled and waved at me. I waved back, but tried to avoid talking to them, because you always ended up going through the same old 'Hello, what is your good name? Where are you from? Are you married?' crap with every single person, and I just couldn't face it any more.

Then, after a few minutes, I spotted another white guy, right up at the front of the train, near the first-class carriages. He was sitting on a rail, looking down the track towards me. Thank God! At last – someone to talk to!

I was almost jumping on the spot with delight, and gave him a huge wave. Although he must have seen my greeting, he didn't acknowledge me, but simply turned his head and looked away, out over the swamp. As I approached him, almost at a run, he still didn't turn towards me, even though he would have heard my feet crunching on the stones.

I sat on the rail next to him, and just his presence by my side made me feel calmer.

'Hi,' I said.

He waited for a while, as if he was hoping that I'd go away, then, eventually, he turned towards me and said hello. Then he looked at me. Properly looked at me. Like he was examining my face for something.

I couldn't think of anything to do other than examine him back. He was quite old – in his mid-thirties or something – and had wiry hair forced down into a side parting, with a dense but short beard. His eyes had a slightly disturbing look in them: glazed over, but still somehow piercing. And he wasn't wearing the usual traveller gear, but was actually dressed in trousers and a shirt.

'Where are you from?' I said.

'Bangalore,' he said, then he watched my reaction. I tried not to have one, but it didn't really work. I wanted to know where he was really from. While I was trying to find a way of asking that wouldn't sound racist, he said, 'Manchester'.

Then, after a while, to fill the gap, he said, 'Reuters'. I nodded slowly, and to finally cement the hole, he said, 'Journalist'.

'Right.'

This was a chatty kind of guy. I wanted to tell him that he'd obviously spent too much of his life writing telegrams and should learn some social skills, but he wasn't the kind of person you could say that to. In fact, he didn't seem to be the kind of person you could say anything to.

It was ages since I'd spoken to a proper . . . you know, adult. Someone with a job. Other than the Indians – they've got jobs, obviously – I just mean someone from back home. A European with a job. Someone doing something real.

This fact somehow made my mind go blank, and I couldn't think of anything to say to him.

Eventually, I said, 'Where are you heading?'

'To cover the strike,' he said.

I nodded, as if this was an answer I understood.

He kept looking at me, so I carried on nodding.

'Do you know which strike I'm talking about?'

'The strike?'

'Yes. The strike.'

'Um . . . I haven't read a paper for a few days, actually.'

He snorted. 'Congress have been arguing with the BJP over Harijan quotas in higher education, and the Maharashtran Sabha has been unable to pull off a conclusive vote against the threatened general strike. It's probably all going to blow up quite soon.'

'Right.' I nodded vociferously.

'Do you know what I'm talking about?'

'Not really, no.'

'Look. I'll start again. Congress . . .'

I tried to arrange my features to say, 'Go on . . .', but

they somehow still had 'What the fuck?' stamped across them.

'Congress?' he said.

'Ummm . . .'

'You don't know what Congress is?'

'Yes I do.'

'What is it?'

'It's . . . the . . . parliament. The Indian parliament.'

'It's not the parliament. Parliament is the Lok Sabha and the Rahja Sabha. Congress is the ruling party.'

'Oh, yeah. Right. Of course. I knew that.'

'So you know about the argument over Harijan quotas?'

'Not exactly.'

'You know who the Harijans are?'

'Yes.'

'Who?'

'They're . . . um . . . the opposition party.'

'Oh my God, this is unbelievable. "Harijan" is the name for the underclass of Indian society. The Untouchables. The people who've probably swept every floor that you have stood on and cleaned every toilet you've shat in since you've been here. *They* are the Harijans – as renamed by a certain Mahatma Gandhi. You've heard of him, perhaps?'

'Yes, thanks,' I said, with attempted sarcasm.

'Probably just seen the film,' he muttered to himself. 'Just forget it. Forget it.'

Then, shaking his head, he gave every impression of forgetting that I was there, and turned his head away. With a vague smile on his lips and a frown playing across his forehead, he stared out at the swamp.

This was a very rude man. I decided that I wasn't going to let myself be humiliated.

'Look,' I said, 'you're a professional journalist. It's your job to know these things. I'm just travelling here. It's only a holiday. I don't have to revise for my holidays. I get enough of that the rest of the year.'

He turned towards me slowly, and muttered, still apparently to himself, 'You don't have to revise for your holidays.'

Was this his idea of a conversation? He was, without a doubt, the most impolite man I had ever met.

After a while, he said it again, slightly louder, with strange emphasis.

'You don't have to *revise* for your holidays.'

'That's right. I don't have to revise for my holidays. Do you have a problem with that?'

'No,' he said, smiling at me. 'I think it's very accurate.'

'Accurate. What do you mean, accurate?'

'University of Life. Year One – Advanced Adventure Playgrounds. Part One Exam – go to the Third World and survive. No revision, interest, intellect or sensitivity required.'

This guy was unbelievable.

'Look. You don't know anything about me. You don't know why I'm here. You don't know what I think. You don't have any interest in why I've decided to come and what it means to me, so you ... you ... you've got no right to make pronouncements about my ... my journey ... and my ... character. Right?'

He nodded, still smiling. 'You're absolutely right. I don't know anything about you. Nothing at all. And yet I turn up here and make judgements about your character right out of the blue. It's terrible.'

He eyed me with an inquisitive look, but I didn't know what he was on about, so I just tried to stare him out.

'You're *absolutely* right. I'm completely ignorant, and yet I come here, sit next to you, spend a few fleeting moments in your company, then go away feeling that I've learned something about you. It's appalling. I shouldn't even have come here. If I'm not interested, I shouldn't have taken up your time.'

'Oh, right, I *see*. Very clever.' I looked away and tried to ignore him.

Down the track, crowds of people were still chatting and smoking, with no apparent sign of the train moving on. Even though I hadn't exactly hit it off with the journalist, I decided to stay put. I wasn't ready to be on my own again.

'I might do an article on you,' he said.

'What?'

'I might write about you.'

'About me? What have you got to say about me?'

'I'm not sure. Tell me – what do you do all day?'

'What do I do?'

'Yes. What does your average day consist of?'

'Are you taking the piss?'

'No. I'm just curious.'

I gave him a suspicious look. 'You know – I'm travelling. I'm a backpacker.'

'But what do you do all day? How come you don't get bored?'

'Bored? You could never get bored here.'

'What do you *do*, though? In each place.'

He looked genuinely interested.

'Well, you get there. Look for a hotel. Hang out there for a bit. Look around town for a few days. Eat. Read. Sleep. Talk to the other travellers. Think about where to go next, then – you know – it's a big hassle to get the tickets for your next journey, so you prepare yourself for that, then bite the bullet, spend a morning queuing for tickets, and the next day you move on.'

'Right. So the most significant and challenging thing you do in each place is to buy the tickets for getting to the next place.'

'No. I didn't say that.'

'Yes you did.'

'Look – forget it. You're obviously only interested in taking the piss, so I don't see why I should help you write your crappy little feature. You'll have to talk to someone a bit more gullible.'

'It's fine. I've got more than enough material already.'

'Like what? What are you going to write about me, then?'

'I think . . . something about how it's not hippies on a spiritual mission who come here any more, just morons on a poverty-tourism adventure holiday. The real point would have to be about how going to India isn't an act of rebellion these days, it's actually a form of conformity for ambitious middle-class kids who want to be able to put something on their CV that shows a bit of initiative. All the top companies want robots with initiative these days, and coming to the Third World is the ideal hoop for you to leap through. You come here and cling to each other as if you're on some kind of extended management-bonding exercise in Epping Forest. Then, having got the nasty business of travel out of the way, you can go home and prove to employers that you're more than ready to settle down for a life of drudgery. I suppose you could call it a modern form of ritual circumcision – it's a badge of suffering you have to wear to be welcomed into the tribe of Britain's future élite. Your kind of travel is all about low horizons dressed up as open-mindedness. You have no interest in India, and no sensitivity for the problems this country is trying to face up to. You also treat Indians with a mixture of contempt and suspicion which is reminiscent of the Victorian colonials. Your presence here, in my opinion, is offensive. The whole lot of you should fuck off back to Surrey.'

'That's . . . that's bollocks. I respect the Indians.'

'Why did you run the whole length of the train to come and talk to me, then? Do you think I'm the only person here who speaks English?'

'No . . . I just wanted a bit of . . . Look – it's easy for you to come out with this kind of PC crap when you stay in cosy expense-account hotels. If you spent a bit of time with real travellers, you'd see that there are a lot of people who try and rip us off. You have to be a bit suspicious. It's basic self-defence.'

'*Real* travellers. You're priceless. I'm going to have to put that in.'

'Forget it. You're not even listening to me. I just think that your kind of . . . of . . . cynicism is really sad. There's a lot more to what I'm doing than you think.'

'Yeah, sure.'

'At least I'm trying. Most people are happy to . . . to stay totally ignorant about the Third World. At least I've come here.'

'And no one could call you ignorant.'

'That's it. I've had enough of this. I'm off.'

I stood up and stomped back towards my compartment. After a reasonable distance had opened up between us, I turned round for one last look at him. 'AND I'M NOT FROM SURREY,' I yelled.

He gave me a huge grin and an enormous wave. 'ENJOY THE REST OF YOUR HOLIDAY!' he shouted. 'DON'T FORGET TO PUT YOUR BIG TRIP DOWN ON THE CV!'

I gave him the finger.

The locomotive soon gave a hoot, and everyone scrambled back on board with the train already crawling into motion. I looked around the compartment for someone to talk to. Determined to prove the journalist wrong, I decided to make an effort with one of the locals. A guy diagonally opposite me had a couple of pens sticking out of his top pocket and looked reasonably educated, so it seemed like a fair assumption that he would speak English. I smiled at him.

'Hello, my friend,' he said.

'Hello,' I said.

'What is your good name?'

'David.'

'Where are you from?'

'England.'

'Are you married?'

'No.'

'What is your profession?'

'I'm a student.'

'Oh, very good.'

Here we go, I thought. Same old crap.

I responded with a few token questions, and before I knew it I was stuck as the audience for a *Mahabharata*-length discourse on the paths taken by his God-knows-how-many-hundred sons through the Indian civil service. This lasted until we arrived in Bombay. He tried to invite me to his house for supper, but I managed to shake him off, saying that I was in a hurry to meet someone.

In Bombay, I only needed to take one sniff of the city to realize that I couldn't face staying, and walked to the nearest travel agent to buy a ticket for the first bus to Goa (quicker than the train at a mere sixteen hours, according to The Book). The bus was due to leave in two hours, actually left in four hours, and took three more hours to reach the edge of Bombay. Once we reached the open road, it was already after midnight, so I decided to try and fall asleep just as the driver put a tape of Hindi musicals on at top volume. This tape played all night, periodically interrupted by me standing up and shouting at him to turn it down. When I did this, everyone on the bus stared at me as if I was mad. Apparently, it was common practice for bus drivers to play music to help keep themselves awake while they drove through the night. At one of our innumerable stops, I bought a box of biscuits from a road-side stall so that I could tear off strips of cardboard in order to improvize a pair of ear-plugs, which, it turned out, didn't make any difference to the noise, kept on falling out, and gave me sore ears. I also ate all the biscuits in one go, just to try and take my mind off things, which made me feel sick. The bus broke down half-way through the following day, and I ended up hitching to Panjim (the capital of Goa) in the back of a truck, with a pile of axles for my seat. In a delirium of anger, frustration, loneliness and arse pain, I just about managed to face the one final leg of the journey, which was to take a local bus out of the city to the beach. I didn't care where it was going, or which resort I ended up in, as long as there was a beach.

I had clearly been wrong about the joys of travelling. Getting from one place to another was, without any doubt at all, the crap bit. The journeys, quite clearly, were not the point – particularly if you tried to do six little-finger-widths of India in one go.

Comfortably numb

The monsoon travels in a wide band northwards through India. As it gets started in the Himalayas, it will be tailing away down at the southern tip of India. I had caught the beginnings of it up north, but now, having travelled one thousand two hundred miles south, I found myself in the middle of the country, in the middle of the monsoon.

I had ended up in one of the largish resorts, called Colva Beach, but at first sight it seemed deserted. There were still plenty of Indians around, but I couldn't really make out any other travellers. And most of the hotels seemed to be closed.

I found one place from The Book that was open and took a room. Even though it was only mid afternoon, I went instantly to bed.

After a monolithic sleep, I woke up well into the next morning and took my first proper look at the place. There were lots of hotels and bars, but mostly with the shutters up. I wandered down a Tarmac street dusted with sand, which led me from the hotel, past a deserted town square and on to the beach.

The beach was amazing. Miles of empty yellow sand, palm trees along the shore, and . . . well, the sea. The sky was overcast, and the air was a little humid, but this really didn't seem like a good enough reason to close the whole place down. Everything looked fine to me. It was beautiful. I could have a great time here. There was nothing wrong with it at all. Apart from the fact that I was the only person there.

I wandered up and down the beach for a while, but it wasn't long before I got bored. Not yawn-bored, more what's-the-point-of-being-alive bored. I sat in the sand, looked out at the ocean and had a good rummage around my emotions. Here I was, in a beautiful place, utterly calm, unwinding after a long and difficult journey, relishing a well-earned rest with no one telling me what to do, no stress, a comfortable and cheap hotel room, and no Indians hassling me. But although I felt more relaxed, satisfied and confident than I had done since landing in India, I also felt more miserable than I could ever remember. An all-embracing loneliness squatted over me and gave me a strange feeling that my whole life was a sham and I was a tosser who didn't have any real friends. I had got what I deserved. Isolation and misery. I was thousands of miles away from anyone who cared about me, and even the people who cared about me probably didn't, because they had no idea where on earth I was. If I died tomorrow, no one would give a toss. And who could blame people for hating me, when I was a selfish, thoughtless, ignorant human being – an arsehole, a coward and a loser.

As I thought about this, I began to detect that a weirdly pleasurable edge had crept into my unhappiness. A faint masochistic thrill had appeared in my self-hatred, tinging the whole thing with a kind of bitter-sweet melancholia.

And when I saw a vision of myself, as if through a movie camera, sitting on this tropical beach, all on my own, with bitter-sweet melancholia etched on my features, I suddenly felt a surge of joy rush through my body. I was fucking cool. The whole scene could have been part of an aftershave advert. This was exactly what you were meant to do on your year off. This was it – this was the moment. I was finding myself.

I suddenly felt so elated that I almost started to cry, which seemed like a strange reaction, because they weren't happy tears, they were what's-the-point-of-being-alive tears. I instantly felt pissed off with myself for having spoilt the big moment by thinking about crying. From being pissed off, it was just a short hop back to being depressed, miserable, and hating myself again.

I decided that emotional rummaging was a bad idea. It didn't really get me anywhere. But at least I'd found myself, which was a bonus.

I spent a week in Goa, since I couldn't face taking on another journey, and gradually discovered that there were a few other travellers around. I never really got very far with any of them, though. None of them were English, and they were all from that slightly older generation who, for some reason, look down on students. I spoke to them all, and on the surface they were friendly enough, but I couldn't help feeling patronized by them.

There was a little gang of Aussie blokes who were quite a good laugh, but they were all well into their twenties, and had an annoyingly macho way of being friendly that I found a bit intimidating. They also immediately assumed that anyone who was my age must be immature, and I kept on spotting them smirking when I spoke, which really got on my nerves. I felt I couldn't really talk about what I'd done, because they'd all been on the road for months and had amazing stories I couldn't possibly compete with – about how they'd got lost in the Thai jungle with heroin smugglers, had fought off kitten-sized cockroaches in an

Indonesian prison, or had done the entire Everest trek dressed in flip-flops and a Bondai Beach T-shirt.

They hadn't swallowed any of the hippie Mother India crap, but had just gone all over Asia acting like Australians and generally drinking lots of beer and having a laugh. Even though I didn't like them, I had to admit that they were pretty cool.

For the first time, I kind of wished that I'd done more travelling. I'd never been jealous of the older travellers before, because most of them were such transparent social failures. The people in their thirties who were still trudging around India had so obviously cocked up their entire lives that there wasn't much to be jealous of. And most travellers seemed to be either my age or of the sad, beardy basket-case generation. It was when you occasionally bumped into the mid-to-late-twenties crowd that things got a bit scary. There was something about them that always made me envious. When they were around, I always felt like a bit of a child. I couldn't relax when I was talking to them, because I was always worried that something naïve would slip out.

There was only one evening in Goa when I really enjoyed myself, and that was when one of the Aussies almost got into a fight with a Swiss hippie. It was quite late, and everyone had been drinking for several hours in the resort's only hang-out: The Jimmy Hendrix Bar Experiance. The Swiss guy was talking at the top of his voice, trying to impress some girl with a story about how he'd risked his life trying to get into Tibet, but how in the end it had proved impossible.

Garth, one of the larger Australians, interrupted him by tapping him on the shoulder. 'Hey – Pinktrousers,' he said, 'could you turn it down a bit. We're trying to play riotous drinking-games over here.'

This made all the Aussies (and me) laugh.

'What is this?' replied the Swiss guy.

'It's just a small thing, but (a) you're talking far too loudly, and (b) you're talking shit.'

'This isn't shit, my friend. I spent a month almost starving in a prison in Golmud after trying to hitch down into Tibet. This is not shit.'

'Listen mate, I don't mean to brag, but any arsehole with two brain cells to rub together knows that the Golmud route has been closed for years. I managed to get into Tibet only a few months ago, using the southern route from Kashgar.'

'That's bullshit. I researched this route, and it has even more police road-blocks than from Golmud.'

'Golmud's got a whole economy running off travellers who want to look as if they've tried to get into Tibet, but can't actually be arsed to try anything dangerous. Anyone who's serious about it goes from Kashgar.'

'Bullshit. I'm perfectly serious about Tibet, but you can't get past the police.'

'Not if you sit around in cosy Golmud and act like you're on some package holiday, doing whatever the police tell you.'

'Golmud is not cosy!'

'If you're a real traveller, you'll use a bit of initiative and take a few educated risks. I hitched a ride with a trucker who knew the location of the road-blocks, and he dropped me off before each one. I trekked round behind the police, and he picked me up on the other side.'

'That's not possible. This takes weeks, and there are no towns to buy food.'

'Damn right it takes weeks, and I lived off porridge which I shared with the driver, but it's possible. If you really want to, you can get to Tibet.'

'You are a lying, stupid Australian. Everyone knows that Tibet is closed to travellers.'

'Sure it is – officially.'

'You're lying. No one would let you stay there.'

'I didn't say I stayed there. I just said I got there.'

'To Lhasa?'

'Sure.'

'You're a bullshitter.'

'It's fucking true, mate, so I suggest you shut up and sit down.'

'You . . . you . . . and I suppose you've been to Burma as well, have you?'

'As it happens, yes. I trekked over the border from Thailand. Stayed a couple of weeks with the mountain rebels.'

'That's easy. I know hundreds of people who've done that. I trekked into Afghanistan and spent a month with the mujahedin.'

'Well, bully for you Mr Pinktrousers. You're a real hero.'

'Don't be sarcastic with me, Australian idiot.'

'Who are you calling an idiot? I'm not the one who couldn't even get into Tibet.'

'If you think I believe this story, then you *are* an idiot.'

'Fuck you.'

'No – fuck you.'

'No – fuck *you*.'

The two of them traded insults for a while longer, with Pinktrousers eventually switching into Swiss German, which is a damn good language for insulting people. They were moments away from a punch-up when one of the Aussies dragged Garth away, thrust a fresh beer bottle into his hand, and told him that he should take a bit more acid.

*

After almost a week of semi-loneliness and mild boredom, I bumped into two English girls on the beach, who were on their summer holiday from Newcastle university. One of them, called Claire, was a bit ugly, but her friend Sam was a genuine bollock-tighteningly sexy woman – and not in an aloof way, either. She honestly didn't seem to realize how staggeringly fit she was. With her cropped black hair, spindly arms, kissable mouth and twinkling green eyes, she must have been either blind or stupid not to fall in love with herself every time she looked in a mirror. After the aloof Australians, it was a relief to find someone of roughly my own age who I could actually talk to – someone willing to sit down and have a proper conversation which didn't revolve around the exchange of life-threatening-situation anecdotes.

It turned out that they were staying at the next resort down, but had already been there for almost a fortnight, and were preparing to make the journey south to Kerala. I immediately chipped in with a prudent half-lie and told them that I was about to go to exactly the same place myself. I didn't want to look like too much of a sad git and give the impression I was desperate to cling on to them, but the truth was that I simply couldn't face doing another big journey on my own. Looking only mildly enthusiastic about the whole idea, they agreed to meet up the following day to go off in search of train tickets. I couldn't tell what they really thought, because I hadn't given them much of an option to turn me down, but I felt reasonably sure that I could make them like me, given enough time.

Goa to Kerala is a long way, and we decided to take a night train to Bangalore, spend a while there, then head onwards when we were ready.

Our train pulled out of Margao station late in the afternoon and was due to arrive in Bangalore around the following lunch-time. I was so relieved to be on a train with the protection of other people that I had to fight with myself to stop the happiness showing through. If I came across as too pleased to be with them, I thought I'd seem a bit of a loser.

I sat on one side of the compartment with Sam, while Claire faced us from the opposite window-seat, slowly dozing off over her book. Sam and I started chatting the instant the train pulled out, and after an hour or so it turned into one of those talk-about-your-family conversations in which you always end up inventing traumas to try and make yourself sound interesting. I described how the person I loved most in the world was my Down's syndrome brother, and how he was far more sensitive to human emotion than anyone else I knew. She talked about her boyfriend (boring), then about her parents and how she couldn't help feeling that their marriage was going through a difficult phase, with her mother possibly having an affair. I nodded and grunted the occasional approval, too dizzy with lust to offer any sensible comments. I mean, if her *mother* was into that kind of thing . . .

After a while, dusk started falling and the view from the train became incredibly beautiful. Endless paddy-fields stretched to the horizon, dotted with children, water buffalo and rice farmers. The scene was bathed in soft light, and there was a wonderfully peaceful atmosphere of people finishing off their day's work and heading home. As the train clattered slowly through village after village, paddy-fields drifted by in an endlessly varied and beautiful jigsaw, with many children waving at us as we passed.

Sam had a dual-headphone Walkman, and she put on Pink Floyd's *Delicate Sound of Thunder*, which we listened to as the sun set. I hadn't heard any music since leaving

England, and the whole experience, with that view, and that album, was genuinely uplifting. While the batteries lasted, I felt that I was bathing in the essence of life.

If you had seen what I saw, you would know that the Indian countryside was designed with a Pink Floyd soundtrack in mind. It really was. When God put together those paddy-fields, he was definitely listening to 'Comfortably Numb.'

Everyone's had it

On our first morning in Bangalore, I got up for an early breakfast, which I planned to eat as slowly as I could in order to make sure that I would be in the dining room when Sam and Claire came down. This would allow me to ask casually what they were up to, then with any luck to spend the day with them, all without coming across as over-keen.

Streams of other travellers came and went, while I sat there over my omelette and tea, waiting for the two girls.

It was almost lunch-time when I finally gave up. Everyone had disappeared from the hotel, so I prepared myself for a boring day on my own in Bangalore. Then, on my way out, I bumped into them.

'Where've you been?' I said, sounding more eager than I intended.

'Oh, we got up early to go to the railway station,' said Claire.

'Right,' I replied, my heart suddenly sinking. 'You bought tickets?'

'Yeah,' said Sam, 'we don't really want to spend any time here.'

I waited for them to tell me where they were off to, but

neither of them said anything. A long and sickly silence opened up.

Sam, blinking with embarrassment and even a hint of pity, eventually spoke. 'What are you up to today, then?'

'Just . . . looking round town.'

I pointed to the bag over my shoulder, as if this explained my point further.

'Right.'

There was another silence.

'Bye,' I said, and wandered off. I didn't even wait for them to answer. As I walked away, I could feel them standing still and guiltily watching me go. I didn't know whether to head right or left when I hit the street, but I just wanted to get out of sight, so I turned on instinct and walked blindly into the crowds.

Suddenly, I didn't want to be in India, I didn't want to be in Bangalore, and I didn't want to be anywhere near Sam or Claire. I had no interest in seeing anything, buying anything, or eating anything. I wanted to be at home. I wanted to watch telly. I wanted Marmite on toast, friends, a sofa, *Match of the Day*, green grass, pubs, frost, and a bed with a duvet.

For a long time I walked without even knowing where I was going. In the back of my mind, I was looking for a place where I'd be able to hide from the crowds and forget how far from home I was. The rest of my brain was filled with the thought that there was still a month to go before I was due to fly back. A whole month.

It was a shock to realize how much my happiness had depended on a couple of people I hardly knew. It wasn't as if I wouldn't be able to see them again, or even as if I didn't know where they were going. They were going to Kerala, and everybody's first stop in Kerala was Cochin. If I wanted to, I could probably even have got a place on the same train as them. But they had clearly made a point of trying to get rid of me. This meant that if I wanted to salvage any pride, I had to spend at least another couple of days in Bangalore and would have to try and ignore them when I got to Cochin. I was still going to go there – that much was certain. I wasn't going to miss out, just because *they* didn't want to see me – no way.

The gutting thing was, I really thought Sam had liked me. The other gutting thing was that Bangalore was a dump. Oh, and there was also the small matter of me being utterly pissed off with the entire continent, and wanting to eat Marmite on toast in front of *Match of the Day* under a frosty duvet on a sofa in a London pub.

Eventually, I stumbled across a restaurant called MacSpeed. I poked my head round the door and saw a kind of Wimpy Burger Bar *à la* 1982, with moulded plastic seats screwed to the floor around tiny Formica tables. I hadn't seen anything remotely like this since . . . well, since 1982, and certainly hadn't spotted any burger restaurants in India.

God was clearly looking down, and had done his best to provide comfort food for depressed, lonely, homesick little me. I ordered a lamb burger and chips (no beef, obviously), with a Campa Cola on the side, and ice-cream for afters. I couldn't even be bothered to worry about what kind of water was in the ice-cream. I was giving myself a treat and would eat exactly what I wanted to cheer myself up.

This was my first meat for weeks, and it tasted absolutely delicious, as did the chips, the Coke (despite a hint of ammonia in the aftertaste) and the ice-cream. If I shut my eyes, I could almost imagine myself back home.

I was three-quarters of the way through my lamb burger when it occurred to me that I'd travelled more than two thousand miles all over the country and had yet to see a single sheep. The question of which animal had been mashed up to produce my burger suddenly became a rather pressing mystery. Whatever it was, it wasn't sheep, and it almost certainly wasn't cow. Precisely which varieties of red meat with burger potential remained, was a difficult one.

Pig? No. It definitely didn't taste of pork.

Goat? Possibly. There were plenty of goats around.

Dog? No. Not dog. Please. Not dog.

Leaving the remaining corner of burger on the side of my plate, I finished the chips and rinsed my mouth thoroughly with the ammonia-flavoured Coke.

On the way back to the hotel, a curious thing happened. I was walking down the street, feeling a touch anxious about my meal, when I suddenly found myself puking in the gutter.

Having voided my stomach, I stood up and looked around self-consciously to see if I had provoked a reaction. A few metres down the road, an emaciated sadhu with grey dreadlocks was meditating on the pavement. On the other side of the street, a fully soaped-up man was washing himself from a bucket of water, and right in front of him a man trying to transport huge bundles of steel on the back of two donkeys was having an argument with a mango-seller who wouldn't move his pile of fruit out of the way.

A vomiting Westerner, apparently, didn't stand out. No one seemed to notice or care what I had done, other than a small dog who trotted over and started lapping up the puddle at my feet. I wiped my mouth with a T-shirt sleeve, and leaving my burger behind for the cannibalistic dog, continued back to the hotel, stopping on the way to buy a bottle of mineral water.

*

That evening, I was standing over the toilet doing a pre-bed piss, when I let a fart escape, only to feel an odd sensation in my boxer shorts. My underwear suddenly felt heavier. This was followed by the sensation of a warm, wet blob sliding down the back of my thigh. Realizing what had happened, I clamped shut my sphincter and dribbled out the remains of my piss. By the time my bladder was empty, the miniature turd had reached the back of my knee.

In a crouched, waddling sprint, I charged out of the toilet and upstairs to my bedroom. Having peeled my clothes off and tossed them on to the floor, I got into the shower and scrubbed my entire body. I then plucked a few of the more soiled clothes from the heap, and rinsed them in the shower. Once I had got most of the loose crap down the plug-hole, I hung my stuff up to dry, so that it would look respectable enough to give in as hotel laundry the following morning.

Later that night, I was woken from deep sleep by a man revving up a Formula One racing car inside my bowels. It took me a few seconds to realize what was happening, before I sprinted to the toilet and shat like I have never shat before.

I don't know if you have ever seen a cricket bowling-machine, but they work by having two small tyres, placed horizontally next to each other, rotating extremely fast in the same direction. A cricket ball rolls towards the two tyres, then becomes gripped between them, and is flung out at up to a hundred miles an hour. Well, imagine what would happen if you set that machine to maximum speed, then poured in a cow-pat. This is the only way I can describe my new experience of shitting.

After this sudden burst of viciously propelled turd, I felt a rancid and acidic stench rise from between my knees. Just as my nose started twitching with revulsion, I noticed that my arsehole was on fire. I couldn't squat for much longer without my hips objecting, so I hurriedly used the Indian arse-wiping technique – dabbing water from a bucket on to the tenderized flesh of my anus.

Only when I was back in bed, having spent at least ten minutes washing my hands, did I begin to realize that my stomach was in agony. I felt as if someone had mistaken it for a soggy flannel and was trying to wring it dry. After writhing naked on the bed for a while, I felt another emergency alarm-call and ran back to the toilet. From the doorway, I noticed that it now wasn't possible to get within striking distance of the porcelain without standing in flecks of my own widely scattered turd. There was little time for squeamishness, however, and certainly not enough time to put my shoes on, so I braved the filth, attempting to replace my feet in the footprints I had left behind.

The second I had squatted, I heard a strange sound of rushing water coming from behind me. 'What's that?' I fleetingly wondered, 'Who could be running a bath at this time of night?' Then I realized that it was me. My numb arsehole had become a tap.

When the gush of liquid had subsided, I toppled forwards, my forehead pressing into the wall in front of me. Still in squatting position, I let out a few groans and attempted to gauge whether or not my punch-drunk sphincter was now closed. It was hard to tell definitively, but I got the impression that even if it was, it would be about as effective as a cat-flap in the Hoover Dam.

When it became too painful to squat, I hauled myself upright, rinsed my legs and feet in the shower and stumbled back to bed. I knew that it was important not to get dehydrated, and since I had just shat out more water than I could remember drinking in the last fortnight, I made myself swallow the remaining half-litre of mineral water from the bottle I had bought that evening.

I felt the liquid slosh around in my belly and knew instantly that it wasn't welcome. After a sudden and vicious stomach cramp, I rushed back to the bathroom just in time to projectile-vomit against the wall of the shower. Even when all the water had come out, my stomach continued its contractions, making me gag on an empty throat.

After this, I didn't have the strength to make it back to my bed. Instead, I turned the shower on, waited for the worst of the vomit to get rinsed away and curled up under the stream of water. I positioned myself so that I wouldn't have to remain anxious about the feeble state of my cat-flap and could simply let any late seepage get washed down the plug-hole.

I had no real sense of time by this stage, but when I eventually felt sure that my body was fully drained, I crawled back to bed and fell asleep.

I was woken by voices in the corridor. The second my eyes were open, I felt the pain return to my throat, stomach and arsehole, but I knew that these voices represented my only chance of contact with the outside world, so I hauled myself out of bed and scrabbled through my rucksack for a clean pair of trousers. Having pulled on some clothes, I rushed into the corridor.

'Hello! Hello!' I croaked, just as the voices disappeared down the stairs. 'Hello!'

There was silence for a second or so, then I saw a head reappear around the corner of the staircase. 'Yes, hello?'

'Please! Come back! I'm sick!' I said, supporting my weight on the door-frame.

He called something down the stairs, in a language that sounded like it was probably Dutch, then wandered towards me.

'What's up?' he said.

'I'm sick! I can't walk! I need some water!'

'What's wrong?'

'Everything. Shitting, puking . . .'

'The usual, then.'

'I suppose so.'

'You want me to buy some water, yes?'

'Please. Thanks. I'd be so grateful. I'll get you some money.'

I hobbled back into the room and came back with a few notes. I saw the beginnings of a smile around the edges of his mouth as he watched me try to walk.

'Does it hurt?' he said.

'Yes. My arsehole's in tatters.'

He laughed and clapped me on the back. 'Hey! We've all been there.'

'It's fucking agony.'

'No, it's not. You wait. If it's food poisoning, you have a chance to be better in a few days. If it's dysentery, you get worse. Then you know what pain feels like. Bacillary dysentery, you have it for a week. Amoebic, and you're fucked.'

He clapped me on the back again.

'You've had dysentery?'

'Yeah, sure. Everyone's had it.'

'What did it feel like?'

'Bad, man. Pretty bad.'

'Which did you have? Amoebic, or . . . the other one.'

'I had both at once, which was a big fucker. Still, even that's not agony. Now malaria, on the other hand. You wait till you get malaria. This is a real bitch. I got it in Nepal and I was so fucked I couldn't get myself to a doctor, so I just had to take a bunch of my Chloroquine and hope for the best.'

'Is that what you're supposed to do? I mean . . . if I . . .'

'I don't know. I'm not expert, but I look on the packet

and read that it has quinine in it, so I just experiment.'

'What do you mean?'

'Well, I took four the first day, then increased the number by one each day until I felt better.'

'H-h-h-how long did that take?'

Suddenly, I seemed to have forgotten my own pain. I was transfixed.

'About ten days.'

'But isn't that stuff supposed to make your hair fall out, and turn you psychotic?'

He suddenly leaped in the air, kicked his legs, stuck his tongue out, whooped and wobbled his hands above his head. This was a terrifying sight, and I felt myself almost wanting to vomit again.

'Not me, I'm fine,' he squeaked, in a manic voice.

With a gasp of relief, I realized that he was joking, and my pulse went back to normal. I forced out a feeble laugh, as a way of indicating to him that he could stop jumping on the spot.

Once he was at rest, he spoke in his normal voice again. 'Hey – even malaria's not the end of the world. The locals live with it.'

'Right.'

'And die of it!' With this, he doubled up with laughter.

Eventually, having calmed down enough to speak, he said, 'Lighten up, man. You've just got a bit of diarrhoea. It's nothing. Drink water and you'll be fine. At least you haven't got this!'

He pulled up his trouser leg and showed me an angry-looking trench gouged out of his skin, just next to the shin-bone.

'What's that?'

'It's from a worm that lives in bad water. It swims through a tiny cut in your skin, or even up the end of your dick, then it grows inside you to a big, big size, living inside your . . . what do you call this?'

'Your veins?'

I felt dizzy.

'Veins. Exactly this. Once the worm gets to be big, you feel the pain, but there's not a sign of it on the surface, and no one can tell what's wrong with you. You have to keep your eyes out, and if you see a lump near the skin which is moving, you must dig with a needle, until you see enough of the worm's head. You can't pull it out all at once because it will snap, and worse than having a live worm in you is having a dead one, so you must put the head around a matchstick, and then give the stick one twist a day, until the whole worm is winding round outside your leg.'

My knees went weak, and a head-rush closed in on my vision. I gripped the door-frame tighter and tried not to listen.

'If the worm gets to your heart, that's it. The end. Paf! I am lucky. I get it out of my leg.'

We both admired the hole in his shin for a second. I felt some strength come back to my thighs and my peripheral vision returning.

'And that's lucky, is it?'

'Yeah, sure.'

'Is it ever going to heal?'

'One day, I hope. There'll be a scar, though.'

'That's good.'

'Eh?'

'Something to show for your efforts, and all that.'

'Oh, no. I kept the worm. I can always use this if I need proof.'

'You carry the worm around with you?'

'No, don't be silly. I post it back to my parents' house.'

'And they're keeping it for you?'

'I ask my mother to pickle it, but I think she's not so keen.'

'Strange, that.'

'Yeah. Look – my friends are waiting. You want me to get you some water?'

'Please. That would be great.'

'You want some food?'

'No. Can't eat.'

'You should.'

'I can't.'

'I'll get you bananas. When you feel stronger, you should eat boiled rice.'

'I couldn't.'

'I'll be back soon. Go to bed.'

'Thank you. You're really kind. You've saved my life.'

'I don't think it's quite this bad.'

'No, really. Thank you. I'm so grateful.' I felt my eyes moistening, and my chest filled with a pressure that wanted to turn itself into a sob.

The guy put his hand on my shoulder. 'You'll be fine,' he said. 'Hey – what's your name?'

I took a deep breath and spoke in a high-pitched, wobbly voice. 'Dave, from England. You?'

'Igor Boog, from Delft in Holland.' He smiled at me and gave my shoulder a squeeze. 'You'll be fine, Dave. I come back soon.'

'Thanks. Really – thanks.'

'It's OK.'

As he wandered away, his sandals clacking against his heels, I called after him, 'Thanks, Igor.'

He laughed and raised a hand to me without turning round. 'Be brave, Dave,' he said and disappeared down the stairs, chuckling.

*

For the next week, I barely left my room. Igor popped in every morning and brought me water, bananas, and after a couple of days, boiled rice. He sat with me while I ate and cheered me up with tales of crippling and life-threatening diseases.

Near the end of the week, just as I polished off my first boiled egg, Igor told me that he'd already extended his stay in Bangalore by a couple of days, and now that I was on the mend, he really had to get going.

I felt myself wanting to cry again.

'OK', I said.

'I have to go, Dave. There's nothing left for me to do in Bangalore.'

'OK. Thanks for everything, anyway. I wouldn't have survived without you.'

'I think you might have done.'

'You saved my life.'

'It wasn't even dysentery, you know.'

'I know, but I'd just had enough of everything, and . . . I mean, I've still had enough of everything, but at least I've got the strength to walk now.'

For some reason this made him laugh.

'You have to be more positive, man. India's a great country.'

'I know, I know.'

'It's the best place in the world.'

'After England.'

'You should try travelling in Africa. In Africa they've this fly which lays its eggs in wet clothes. When the eggs feel the warmth of a body, they hatch into tiny maggots which wriggle through your skin and start to grow inside you. You can only get them out by rubbing Vaseline . . .'

'Please, Igor. I'm not in the mood today.'

'I'm just trying to cheer you up.'

'I know, I just . . . feel a bit weak. I really am on my own once you've gone. I've got some friends in Cochin, but I'll never catch up with them now, and it's all just a bit shit at the moment.'

'Dave – you were ill, now you're better. So be happy.'

'You're right.'

'I'm not going to be here to tell you funny stories any more, so you have to take a positive attitude.'

'You're right.'

'You have to do it on your own now.'

'OK. And thanks for everything. I mean – for staying behind to help me. Most people aren't kind enough to . . . I mean, they wouldn't . . . and you . . . you . . .' I had to stop, or I would have burst into tears.

Igor squeezed my arm, and I started to sob.

'Come on, tough guy,' he said.

'Sorry. I don't mean it. I'm just grateful, that's all.'

'Hey – it was nothing. Anyone would have done the same.' He passed me a corner of the sheet to wipe my face.

'You're very kind.'

'No problem. Really.'

He smiled at me, obviously trying to gauge whether I had calmed down enough for him to make an exit.

While I snivelled, he patted my leg through the sheet and eyed the door.

'I want to go home, Igor. I WANT TO GO HOME!'

His face fell.

'You'll be fine soon. You just need to get your strength back.'

'I WANT TO GO HOME!'

'Go, then. If you want to go home, you can.'

'I can't.'

'You can.'

'I can't. There's still three weeks on my ticket.'

'Then change it.'

'I can't.'

'You can.'

'I can't. It's . . . it's a wadyoucallit.'

'Apex?'

'That's it.'

'You can still change it. You just have to pay.'

'I can't.'

'Why not?'

'I just can't.'

'Why? You can't afford it?'

'I don't know.'

'How much money do you have left?'

'About five hundred pounds.'

'What's that? Seven hundred dollars?'

'I suppose so.'

'Then you can go home. Even if you buy a new ticket you have enough to go home.'

'I can't, though.'

'Why not?'

'Because.'

'Because what?'

'Just because.'

'Why?'

'Because it's embarrassing.'

'Aaahh, so this is it. If you go home early, you'll feel like you've given up.'

'Exactly.'

'You'll feel like you've failed the test.'

'I've done over two months – I've almost finished. It's stupid to give up now.'

'It's not meant to be a strength test, you know.'

'What else is it, then?'

'A holiday?'

'It's not a holiday. It's travelling. They're completely different.'

'Well, why don't you stay, and try to turn it into a holiday? Then you have some fun. Go to one of these stupid resorts where people just hang out on the beach and forget they're in India. Why don't you sit the rest of your time on the beach in Goa?'

'I've just come from Goa.'

'There's other places the same. You could go to Kovalam. Or Ajmer.'

'That's where I was before Goa.'

'And now you've had enough of India?'

'Yes.'

'But it doesn't seem like you've seen any of it.'

'I don't care. I'm sick of India.'

For the first time since I had known him, Igor went silent.

'You think I'm stupid,' I said.

He shrugged.

'You do. You think I'm stupid.'

'Not stupid. Just young. Too young.'

'For what?'

'For this country.'

'There are Indians much younger than me.'

He laughed. 'But they live here.'

'So?'

'Dave – I have to go.'

'OK.'

'I'm going now.'

'Go, then.'

'Bye, Dave. All the best.'

'Bye. And thanks.'

'Have fun, yeah?'

'Yeah.'

He walked out of the room and closed the door without

even looking back at me. It seemed a shame to part like that, but I couldn't really help it. I didn't want to be abandoned again, and I found it hard to be magnanimous.

After staring at the closed door for a few hours, I decided that the time had come for a taste of the outside world. It took me a while to locate my shoes, which were next to the toilet where I had taken them off a week ago.

On wobbly legs, I headed down the corridor, through the hotel lobby and out into the devastatingly bright sun.

Most educative

I tottered across the road, and after a brief wander I was so tired that I sat on the kerb to rest. It was a good spot for watching the world go by, and I was soon joined by an oldish man, who came and sat next to me.

'Would you believe me if I told you that before partition most of my playmates were British citizens,' he said.

He looked like he was probably a bit of a boring old duffer, and normally I would have blanked him, but for once I was pleased to have someone to talk to, and tried to think of a friendly response.

'Really? That's . . . um, impressive.' I said.

'Oh, most assuredly. Johnny, Peter and Freddie were the names of my three closest chums. Of course, they all departed after 1947.'

'All of them?'

'Partition, old chap. A lot of good eggs decamped pretty sharpish.'

'That's terrible. And . . . er, why did you have so many English friends?'

'British, old boy. One mustn't forget our Caledonian compatriots. Freddie was a Scot, you see.'

'Oh, right. But why were they all . . . ?'

'My dear departed father, God rest his soul, was a pillar of the church. And I in my turn have had the good fortune to follow in his footsteps. Are you a Christian?'

I toyed with the idea of telling him that I was an Arsenal supporter instead, but decided that it would be more tactful to lie.

'Yes.'

'C of E?'

I couldn't quite remember what C of E stood for, but it was obvious that he wanted me to say yes, so I nodded.

'Marvellous. What a happy coincidence. Allow me to introduce myself – Charles A. Tripathi, junior.'

He shook my hand.

'I'm Dave. David.'

'Delighted to meet you. Do you take tea?'

'Um . . . I suppose so.'

'Come to my house. It isn't pleasant to be alone.' I didn't know whether this referred to me or to him, but I obeyed and followed him down the street. He turned off down a side-road, marching a few steps ahead of me and making no effort to converse.

Just as I was beginning to feel that I couldn't go much further, we arrived at a tiny concrete house. He stood at the door and ushered me in.

As I entered, it occurred to me that this was the first home I had seen since arriving in India. I was surprised by how much it looked like an English one: TV set in the corner, a few chairs, a rug, pictures on the wall. Everything seemed pretty recognizable, really.

'Sit, please,' he said, indicating a chair. 'Feel free to examine some of our literature.' He pointed at a pile of leaflets on a coffee-table, then left the room.

I could hear him shouting things in Hindi, so I picked up a leaflet and started reading. The colours and typeface made it look like it had been printed in the seventies. On the front it said *South India Christian Mission: An Introduction*. Below that was a whole load of text that I couldn't be bothered to read, so I opened it up, revealing three pictures on three pages, each with a large caption at the top. On the left, it said, 'KNOWLEDGE' above a picture of a wise old man with a grey beard; in the middle, it said, 'BEAUTY' above a picture of a butterfly; and on the right, it said, 'STRENGTH' above a picture of a nuclear mushroom-cloud.

I was in the process of retrieving my jaw from the coffee-table when Charles returned with a child dressed in rags. He shouted something at the kid, who started sweeping the floor under my feet with a long bundle of twigs. On another command, the kid ran out of the room.

'Tea and cakes will be arriving presently,' said Charles.

He remained standing and hovered around me nervously, while I sat in the chair fiddling with the leaflet, trying to think of something to say.

After a while, seven or so smartly dressed children bundled into the room, pushing and shoving at each other to get a good view of me without getting too close.

'These are my grandchildren. And if you don't mind, they would like your autograph.'

'My autograph?'

'Exactly. A sample of your handwriting will be most educative.'

I didn't have the heart to tell him that my handwriting had been bad at the age of ten, and in steady decline ever since. He passed me a pen and said something to them in Hindi. One by one, they came up to me and gave me a scrap of paper. I wrote my name and a little message for each of them, as neatly as I could, and gave each child a pat on the head.

The children then trooped out of the room and ran into the street, laughing.

'You are a very kind man,' said Charles. 'I can tell already. Above and beyond the call of duty – this is your motto.'

'Um . . . I suppose it is.'

'And modest, too, of course. English schooling is still the best in the world, I am pleased to see.'

'I'm not sure about that, you know.'

'Come, come. You have made your point already. Grammar school or public school, I don't even want to know which one. You have the mark of a gentleman stamped all over you.'

'Thank you very much. And may I be permitted to say the same of you.'

Christ! I was beginning to talk like him.

'I try my best. I try my best.'

At this point an old woman entered, carrying a tray of tea and some cakes so lurid it made my teeth ache just to look at them. She placed the tray in front of me, and retreated to the doorway.

'My wife,' said Charles.

'Pleased to meet you,' I said, with a little wave.

'*Namaste,*' she said, nodding and smiling.

I nodded and smiled back at her, then she left.

After this, Charles and I slowly ran out of conversation. I tried to ask about his family and his work, but I didn't really get very much out of him. He kept giving short, awkward answers, as if my questions were either rude or boring. I knew this was my big chance to find out what it's actually like to be an Indian, but I somehow never got very far.

When my attempt at conversation had run aground, he took over, and inflicted the usual job/marriage/home questions on me. After that he bombarded me with endless inane crap about his position in the church and the success of the South India Mission. It was impossible to leave, and only when I was climbing the walls with boredom did I finally get out of his house.

Although we hadn't really managed much of a conversation, and I'd been mostly bored out of my skull, I felt that the visit marked a significant and positive watershed. I had actually gone inside an Indian house. Gone inside, sat down and talked to a real Indian person.

Throughout my entire two-month stay, I'd been tantalized by occasional glimpses into people's houses and had always wondered what it really looked like inside. Previously, I'd never been able to get beyond the odd glance through a window or door, but now I'd actually broken through. I had seen the real India. I had discovered how people lived.

Suddenly, everything else I had done in India seemed totally superficial. I'd just sat around in hotels and talked to other travellers. I'd been wasting my time. Igor was right – I hadn't actually seen *anything*. From now on, I decided, things were going to be different. I was going to stay on my own. I wasn't going to look for other Westerners to hide behind. I was going to make an effort to talk to Indians. I'd befriend them and try to get into their houses. I would make myself into a proper traveller.

India does that to you

That evening I ate my first proper meal since the dog-burger. A couple of months ago I would have been unlikely to describe squidgy lentils dribbled over a lump of coagulated rice as a proper meal, but in the context, this was the most challenging thing my guts had attempted for quite some time.

After a few grumbles of objection, I felt my stomach reluctantly accept the extra workload. My food no longer seemed to float inside me, ready to hurl itself out of my mouth at a moment's notice, but actually settled down and gave the impression that it was willing to be digested. If I could just get the passing-through time to more than ten minutes, I felt I might be able to derive enough benefit from my food to begin to get some strength back.

After having eaten as much as I could force down, I scanned the hotel dining room for someone to talk to. People came and went, but I couldn't help feeling that everyone was ignoring me. I sat there for at least an hour, desperate for someone to talk to, but whenever I caught anyone's eye, they looked away before I had time to say anything.

This was extremely puzzling until, on the way to bed, I caught sight of myself in a mirror. I looked like one of those comatose skeletons I'd seen on my first day in Delhi.

My cheeks had caved in and were covered with long, tufty stubble, my eyes were dead, my hair was greasy, and my mouth was stuck in a sour downward curve. I looked like hell. *I* would have run away from me.

I went to bed and stared blankly into space for a few hours.

I really had turned into one of the living dead.

Despite my 'meal', I slept through the entire night without any emergency trips to the toilet and woke up the next morning resolved to stuff myself with food until I looked like a human being again.

I still didn't trust any greasy or spicy food to stay down, so I had four boiled eggs and a couple of chapatis for breakfast, then set out on my mission to make friends with the subcontinent.

I wandered around for a bit, smiling at everyone, but it didn't seem to make anyone want to talk to me. Remembering that I looked like a Moonie, I toned down the smiles a fraction, but people still avoided me.

Feeling dispirited, I went into the busiest restaurant I could find for a bite of lunch. I sat down next to a lonely looking man, smiled at him and said hello. He picked up his tray of food and walked to a different table, looking mildly frightened.

This represented a new low. To be abandoned by other travellers was one thing, but to be shunned by Indians – that was just the pits. In desperation, back at the hotel I tried to start a conversation with the boy whose job it was to sweep the floor. He ran away.

The only thing left to do was to write a postcard.

Dear Mum & Dad,
I'm now in Bangalore – the modern, industrialized capital of Karnataka. It's a relatively pleasant city, and feels more prosperous than most

other towns I've visited. I haven't actually seen much of it yet, though, because for the last week or so I've been violently ill and haven't left my hotel room. I can just about walk again now, and today I went on my first little excursion. I seem to have lost loads of weight, but I'm sure I'll get it back eventually. I'm still missing you and feeling terribly lonely, but have changed all my ideas about travel, and am now resolved to stay on my own until the end of the trip. Travel shouldn't be about other travellers — it is about India and Indians. If you want to find yourself in this country, you have to lose yourself. This is my next step. I really am learning an incredible amount.

love,
Dave

Having finished the postcard, it dawned on me that even if no one else was willing to have a conversation with me, the hotel receptionist would have to. It was his job, for God's sake. I was paying for a room in his hotel. If I cornered him at the reception desk, he wouldn't be able to run away, and I'd be certain to get a small amount of conversation out of him.

Having waited for him to take his place behind the desk, I engaged in a surprise attack.

'Hello,' I said.

'Hello, sir,' he replied.

I couldn't think of anything else to say.

'Is everything all right?' he said.

'Fine, thanks. Yes.'

I still couldn't think of anything. Then a thought dawned on me.

'It's hot today,' I said.

'Yes. Very hot. Less hot than usual, of course. But hot.'

I was just about to give up when an Indian man walked in, with a cotton scarf wrapped around his head and neck, also covering half of his face. He approached the desk and asked for a room in a heavy South London accent. The minute I heard that voice, I knew who it was.

'Ranj!' I screamed.

He spun round and looked at me suspiciously. After a few seconds, I saw recognition dawn, and he tore the scarf from his head.

'Dave! Is it you?'

'Of course it's me.'

'What the fuck happened to you?'

'I've been stuck here. I got a bit ill.'

'You look like shit. You look like a piece of shit.'

'Thanks, mate.'

'I hardly recognized you. Jesus – have you weighed yourself?'

'No.'

'Have you been to a doctor?'

'No. I don't need to now. I'm on the mend.'

'Fuckin'ell. That's good to hear, man. You look absolutely fucked.'

'I tell you, I'm glad to see you.'

'Likewise, man. Likewise. Where's . . . whatsername. The fit one.'

'We separated. Irreconcilable differences and all that.'

'She left you then.'

'Sort of. We just . . . kind of started off on the wrong foot anyway, and I can't really remember how, but we ended up hating each other's guts.'

'Bad news, man. India does that to you.'

'We always got on fine in England.'

'Me too. I always got on OK with my family in England. Now they all want to kill me.'

'You ran away again?'

'Yeah. I've just flown in from Delhi today. I wanted to get down to Trivandrum, but there were no flights, so I came here.'

'They'll be gutted. I struck up quite a friendship with your brother.'

'And it's worse this time, because . . .' he lowered his voice and looked around the room '. . . I nicked a load of credit cards and cash before I left.'

'From who?'

'Uncles and shit. They were just getting on my tits too much.'

'Really?'

'Yeah.'

'You nicked from your own family.'

'Yeah, I know, I know. I regret it a bit now. I've decided I'm going to spend it all as fast as I can, then go back and apologize.'

'That's very moral of you.'

'D'you think so?'

'No. Not really. Look – d'you want to share my room? It's a double anyway, and it'll be cheaper if we go halves. I could do with some company.'

'Fuck cheaper. I'm living on borrowed time before I get strung up by the balls. I only came to this shitty little hole because it was the first one in The Book. I'm spending one night here, then I'm off to Kovalam.'

'What's in Kovalam?'

'Girls, man. Girls on package tours. It's like Goa, but with less hippies, and the season's about to start. It's right down south, so the monsoon's almost finished. I'm going to check myself into a posh hotel and screw as many white girls as I can before it's too late.'

'Too late for what?'

'Oh, that's what started all this shit off. My dad's trying to marry me off to this tight-arsed virgin bitch, just because her dad owns the Bombay stock exchange or some other crap like that. He's not letting me go home until I've said yes.'

'Jesus! What are you going to do?'

'I've said yes already. There's nothing I can do about it. I said yes, then I pissed off.'

'With your uncle's money.'

'Right. It's the least I deserve. Look – d'you want to come with me? I'll pay for your room. We can have a laugh. If you buy some clothes, eat a bit of decent food and have a shave, you'll look reasonably presentable. We could do pretty well, me and you. My cousin's told me about this excellent hotel where all the loosest women go. What d'you reckon?'

'What?'

'Do you want to come?'

'Are you serious?'

'Course I am. Are you on for it?'

'Er . . . why not? Sounds like a laugh.'

'Cool. I'll send a boy to get train tickets, you go for a shave, and I'll meet you back here later.'

'All right. You sharing my room, then?'

'Thanks, but no thanks. Sick rooms aren't really my scene.'

Golf?

The journey to Trivandrum took ages, but Ranj bought a couple of water-melons, a bag of mangos, several bunches of bananas, a kilo of mixed nuts and an endless supply of Bombay Mix, all of which went a considerable way to helping the time pass. We shared our compartment with a family who were carrying even more food than Ranj, and with everything getting passed around, the whole thing felt more like a banquet than a journey. No one in the family spoke any English, and Ranj couldn't communicate with them either due to some problem with dialects, but this didn't seem to stop them from wanting us to consume vast quantities of their food.

I had to go easy on the fruit, for obvious reasons, but there were plenty of other things to eat, most of which I stuffed down with glee. The sheer relief of finding myself back on the road without being alone had brought about a sudden return to full appetite.

For the first time since Manali, I was properly happy.

From Trivandrum, we got a bus to Kovalam. On the way, Ranj started reading aloud from his copy of The Book.

'What do you think of this? "The most luxurious place to stay is the Kovalam Ashok Beach Resort, on the headland just above the bus terminal. Studio rooms and cottages are Rs 550 single and Rs 650 double. The hotel has every facility you would expect, including air-conditioning, swimming pool, bar, crafts shop and boats for hire. Beautiful place blah blah blah facilities for yoga, ayurvedic massage, golf, tennis, blah blah etc." What d'you reckon?'

'Six hundred and fifty rupees? Are you mad?'

'I'm not getting a double. How are we going to get the shags in if we're in a double? We're talking five fifty each, man.'

'Are you serious?'

'Sure.'

'And you're paying?'

'Yup.'

'Swimming pool and air-conditioning?'

'Yup.'

'*Golf?*'

'Yup.'

'Let's have a look.'

'Nope.'

And with that, he threw his Book out of the bus window.

'What . . . what are you doing?'

'We don't need that any more. We're on holiday now.'

'But . . . but . . . How are we . . . ?'

'Calm down, man. It's only a book.'

'But . . .'

I was in shock. The blood had drained from my face.

'Relax. I haven't thrown away your copy.'

'But . . .'

'I'm saving that to wipe my arse on.'

'Jesus! You've gone mad!'

'You're acting like I've killed someone.'

'You have. Not literally. I mean, how . . . if you don't have The Book, then you don't know where all the other travellers are. How do you expect to meet up with other travellers?'

'On the beach, maybe.'

'But what about . . . ?'

'Besides, we're not looking for other travellers. Who wants to get into bed with some dry-pussied uptight middle-class bitch who can't come and won't suck cock. I mean, for fuck's sake. Raise your horizons a bit, man. We are looking for sex-starved divorcees with twenty years of prime shagging experience stored up in their vaginal muscles and a five-year drought which is just begging to be blasted away by the biggest fucking thunderstorm of their whole damn fucking lives!'

He was jiggling around in his seat, slobbering with antici-pation.

'You could have a point. I've never done it with an older woman.'

He stared into space, his eyes glazed over, and mumbled to himself, 'Jesus Christ! This is going to be fantastic.'

South London was clearly a randy place.

I've got breeding

The hotel was initially reluctant to let me in, and only when Ranj had displayed a wad of cash would they give me a room.

A porter took my rucksack and tried to carry it like a suitcase. This made it almost impossible for him to walk, which Ranj and I found particularly funny, but he just about managed to usher us into a lift and show us upstairs.

A lift! This was incredible. And my room was amazing. I had got used to the idea of a hotel room having grey concrete walls, a stone floor and a rock-hard bed, but this one had a proper bed like in England, a carpet, a balcony overlooking the sea, and even some furniture! It was a single room, but the bed, I noticed, was more than wide enough for two. And there was an *en suite* bathroom which contained the first bath I had seen in the whole country. This was even better than Marmite on toast! I immediately filled it and stripped off.

The water turned grey almost as soon as I had sat in it, so I drained the bath without getting out and ran a fresh one. Having soaked off most of the grime, I met up with Ranj in the lobby. He immediately took me out in a taxi to buy 'some decent clothes'. Since he was paying, I didn't really feel I could argue with his taste, and I ended up wearing a Hawaiian shirt, a pair of lemon-yellow shorts, and blue deck-shoes. He also made me buy evening wear, which consisted of three shirts (all lurid, made of shiny polyester and strangely tight under the armpits), and a pair of ludicrously expensive imitation Levi's which crawled so far up my arse they made my eyes water.

When I was all kitted out, he clapped me admiringly on both arms, and told me that I looked like a proper Indian Playboy.

'Is that good?'

'Of course it's good.'

'Is that what you are?'

'No, man. I'm the Putney Penile Pile-Driver. But you can't buy Putney Pile-Driving gear out here, so we're going to have to settle for Indian Playboy.'

'I feel a bit of a twat.'

'What do you mean, you feel a bit of a twat? How did you feel in this crap?' He pointed to the bag containing my old clothes, which I had refused to throw away.

'I felt fine.'

'Well, you looked like a beggar. Where did you buy that shit?'

'Around. I got most of it in Manali and Dharamsala.'

'I should have guessed. Is this because you thought that wearing Tibetan clothes would help you look like a local in South India?'

'No.'

'Why, then? Why do you people have to wear those disgusting clothes?'

'I don't know. I've got a pair of jeans and a T-shirt at the bottom of my rucksack, but when I arrived and started wearing them I just felt totally out of place. So I bought the same kind of stuff that all the other travellers were wearing.'

'You've got a pair of jeans at the bottom of your rucksack?'

'Yeah.'

'What make?'

'Levi's, I think.'

'You've got a pair of Levi's in the bottom of your rucksack?'

'Yeah. I haven't worn them since I arrived, though. No one wears jeans in India.'

'What are you talking about? Everyone wears jeans in India.'

'No they don't.'

'Yes they do. Why the fuck did you let me buy this imitation shit, when you've got the real thing in your bag?'

'I don't know. I forgot I had them.'

'Do you realize how much you could sell a real pair of Levi's for here?'

'No.'

'Lots. They're gold dust. I can't believe you carry around a pair of Levi's on your back and walk the streets in twenty-rupee peasant trousers.'

'They weren't twenty rupees. They were fifty rupees.'

'You paid fifty rupees for *those*! Fucking hell. It gets worse.'

When Ranj smelled my Levi's he almost choked. He immediately filled my rucksack with every piece of clothing I owned and sent the whole lot down as hotel laundry. I then dressed up in my new evening gear, and we went out on the pull.

The hotel bar was like something out of a James Bond movie, and in honour of the man himself, we each had a dry Martini. Most of the people in the bar were rich Indians, which I had always thought was a contradiction in terms, but there was one corner where all the whiteys were hanging out, and we went over to join them.

Within minutes, I'd dragged Ranj back to the bar for an earful.

'What the fuck are we doing here, man? They're all wrinklies.'

'So?'

'Just look at them. They're repulsive.'

'What d'you expect rich divorcees to look like. Nubile twenty-two-year-old divorcees just don't exist, you know. You might find the odd widow if you're incredibly lucky, but divorcees are old.'

'And that's what you're after? Them?'

'Actually, I have to admit they are a bit ugly.'

'They're dogs. And none of them are even divorced, for God's sake – they're all couples.'

'All right, all right. I'm not clairvoyant. I didn't know who'd be staying here, did I?'

'The only one I fancy is the blonde one over there.'

'The blonde one?'

'Yeah.'

'In the corner?'

'Yeah.'

'With the big guy.'

'Yeah.'

'The one who was just going on about what an idyllic spot this was for a honeymoon.'

'Yeah.'

'Dream on, mate.'

'Well who else is there, for God's sake?'

'She's all right.'

Ranj nodded towards an Indian girl standing near the bar.

'*Her*?'

'Yeah.'

'She's *Indian*!'

'So.'

'You can't chat up Indians.'

'Why not?'

'Just . . . they're . . . I mean, she's with her parents.'

'So?'

'Her brothers will come and kill you in the middle of the night.'

'What for?'

'For . . . insulting her honour, or something.'

'Where do you think you are? Pakistan or something? This is a civilized country.'

'I know.'

'How do you think the race propagates in this part of the world?'

'Just . . . I don't know. You said yourself that you were going to have an arranged marriage.'

'So. Now I'm going to arrange myself a one-night stand.'

'But . . . do they give? Do they put out?'

'Who?'

'Indian girls.'

'Not for you they wouldn't. But remember – I've got breeding.'

And with that, he smoothed his eyebrows and stalked off.

That night, I was woken up by noises coming from Ranj's room which resembled the sound of two people both winning the World Cup in the last minute of extra time with a shot from the half-way line. To my great relief, I soon discovered that you can get satellite pornography on Indian TV.

*

The following morning, he informed me that she'd been a bit young for his taste, but was a reasonable performer anyway. He then politely enquired whether I'd enjoyed my evening's game of bridge.'

'Sod off. It wasn't bridge.'

'What was it, then?'

'Whist.'

'Fair enough.'

'And it was piss-boring. I'm not going to get anywhere if we just hang around in this hotel, you know.'

'It's all right. I've got a plan.'

'What?'

'We hire the hotel boat and cruise the beach.'

'I dunno . . . I've never rowed before. I don't think we'd look too cool.'

'It's not a rowing boat, you arsehole. It's a speedboat.'

'A speedboat? Really?'

'Yeah.'

'A speedboat? That's superb. I've never been in a speedboat.'

'You haven't been in a speedboat *or* a rowing boat?'

'No.'

'What boats *have* you been in?'

'Um . . . a ferry. That's about it.'

'You're a glamorous guy, Dave. You know that?'

'Tell me about it.'

Ping

Ranj seemed to know exactly how to drive a speedboat, even though he claimed that he'd never done it before. We took some cocktails with us, just so we could look even more like James Bond, and did a few lengths of the beach with me leaning out of the side of the boat and screaming for joy. I'd never been so happy in my life. Within a week I seemed to have gone from one of the lowest lows of my life to . . . to actually *being* Sean Connery. Not that Sean tends to whoop with happiness – but you know what I mean.

We couldn't get close enough to the beach to really size up the talent on offer, so we disembarked at one end and took our cocktails for a prowl. Ranj seemed to have a kind of sexual radar which could detect women from huge distances, and as the signals got stronger, he almost went into a trance.

'I can feel something good. There's something good coming. Eyes left. Eyes left.' He was almost running now, and with my feet sinking into the hot sand, I struggled to keep up.

Then Ranj stopped dead, and I almost bumped into him.

'Bingo. Seven blondes.'

'Where?'

'There.'

'Where?'

'By the water. Down there.'

'Can we have a rest? I can't walk that far.'

'Shit – look at that!'

'What?'

'Those two.'

He pointed inland, and I saw two Europeans in the middle distance, dressed in white saris, sitting in the shade. I realized that amongst all the women I'd seen in the whole country, I'd never seen a white sari before. I'd also never seen any Westerners in saris, so it was a strange sight. I couldn't quite make out their faces, but there was something vaguely familiar about them.

'That's weird, that is,' he said.

'I think I recognize them.'

'You know what a white sari means?'

'No.'

'It's like wearing black in England.'

'What – for mourning?'

'Yeah. Widows have to wear white – it symbolizes giving up on worldly pleasures and all that shit.'

'D'you reckon . . . ?'

'She's smoking a joint. She's dressed up like that and she's smoking a joint.'

'I really think I recognize them.'

'It's spooky. That gives me the shivers, that does.'

'I'm going to have a look.'

'Suit yourself. I'm off down there to check out the babes.'

As I got closer and the faces became more distinct, I realized that the two girls were Fee and Caz. And they both looked like death: even thinner than before, with pale, blotchy skin and greasy hair. When Fee saw me approach, she did a huge double take.

'Oh, my God!' she said. 'It's you!'

'Yup.'

She stared at me with a look of horrified revulsion.

'What happened to you?'

I was about to say that I'd got ill when I realized that she was referring to my Hawaiian shirt and lemon-yellow shorts, my cocktail and the snorkelling gear hanging round my neck.

'Oh, you know. The usual,' I said.

She didn't know how to answer that one.

'But . . . what are you doing here?'

'Just – you know. Hanging out. What about you?'

'Same, really.'

Caz, I noticed, was sitting bolt upright in the sand, staring into the middle distance and rocking backwards and forwards like an autistic child. She still hadn't looked at me or even, apparently, noticed my presence.

'Is she all right?' I said.

'No. As it happens, she isn't,' said Fee, in a tone of voice which seemed to imply that I was to blame.

'This is the most incredible coincidence. What are you doing all the way down here? I thought you were on an ashram with Whatsername.'

'Whatsername, as you so rightly call her, is not in our good books.'

'What d'she do?'

'It's a long story.'

'I've got time,' I said, sitting down in the sand, and registering that Ranj had already infiltrated himself into the group of blonde bathers. Caz was still rocking and staring out to sea.

I could tell that Fee was wound tight with stress, and

though she didn't want to admit it, she was obviously pleased to see me. She stared at me for a while, puffing on her joint, before passing it over and beginning her story.

'It all comes down to this guy. He's called Ping . . .'

'Ping?'

'. . . and he's the teacher of Intimate Yoga on our ashram. Anyway – we've been there twice before, and this was our third visit of the year, and each time we've been, Caz has developed more and more of a thing with Ping. Anyway – this time, we take Whatsername with us, *introduce* her to Ping – and it's not as if she doesn't already know about the Caz-and-Ping thing – and . . . and . . . I can't go on.'

She went silent and stared into space with her lips pursed.

'What happened?'

'Well – to cut a long story short, we were in an Intimate Yoga lesson, and Ping was helping Liz . . . I mean, Whatsername . . . to locate her centre, when Liz starts moaning in a completely inappropriate way for a novice. I mean, she was obviously faking. We'd only been there a week. Anyway – Whatsername starts moaning like a cheap slut, and the pair of them just stand up, hold hands and walk out. Now – because Caz can sense Ping's moods, she knows exactly what's going on and she waits a few minutes then goes to the private-tuition room. And . . . and . . . I can't go on.'

There was a long pause.

'And. What?' I said, eventually.

'Well – imagine Caz's surprise when she pokes her head round the door and discovers that . . . that . . . they've gone Tantric.'

'I'm sorry?'

'They've gone . . . Tantric.'

'What's that mean?'

'You don't know what Tantric is?'

'No.'

'Tantric meditation?'

'No.'

'Well, there are sixteen chief meditative states, and each of the five main schools of thought divides the sixteen into three main categories. The Red Hat and Yellow Hat Tibetan schools follow a basic subdivision . . .'

'Please. Forget the other fifteen. Just tell me what Tantric means.'

'It's not one of the sixteen, silly. It's a whole school. It's one of the five.'

'Fine. Are you going to tell me what it is now?'

'It's very hard to encapsulate in a sentence, but it's basically the striving for nirvana through the ultimate centring of the sexual self.'

'What?'

'Basically, you meditate by having sex.'

'So when you say that Liz and Ping had gone Tantric, you mean that they were shagging.'

'That's one way of putting it.'

'Jesus! That's unbelievable! You took her to this place, and within a week she fucked the Yoga teacher.'

'Do you have to be so crude? The point is, Caz is on a bit of a knife-edge at the best of times, and the whole thing just tipped her over.'

'Over what?'

'She had a collapse. Just – oh, it was terrible. She saw the Tantric going on and started screaming and smashing things. Then she took all her clothes off and ran around the entire compound, saying offensive things about the usefulness of meditation. Eventually, one of the spiritual helpers had to put her in a strait-jacket.'

'A strait-jacket?'

'She's fine now, though. I mean, she's not *fine*. She still hasn't spoken or anything. But she's not dangerous or anything.'

'That's awful. How come they've got strait-jackets in this place?'

'Oh, apparently it's quite common. The pressures of a strict Yogic regime can get to some people. There's nothing wrong with Caz, you know. She just needed a rest. So after we got thrown out of the compound . . .'

'They threw you out?'

'Of course. You can't have mad people running around when you're trying to meditate, you know. It's for the good of everyone. Anyway – I decided to fly her down here so she could just relax on the beach, away from all the crowds. Then, once she's got her faculty of speech back, I'm going to take her home. I think if we went home like this, it would upset her parents.'

'Right. This is . . . it's terrible.'

'I know.'

'I mean, she looks like a zombie.'

'Yeah, and we've both got to start university in . . . in around a month.'

'Shit.'

'A bit over, actually. I mean it's going to be hard enough for *me* to get reacclimatized to Western culture. Just the thought of wearing Western clothes makes me feel all itchy – they're so restrictive, you know – but for Caz . . . I don't know.'

'What's she meant to be studying?'

'French and Spanish at Bristol.'

'How's she going to do that when she can't even speak?'

'It'll take a while, but she'll be fine. When you've been living with lepers, this kind of thing seems like nothing. I mean, you've got to put things in a proper perspective.

She's still got more than any Indian could possibly wish for.'

'That's rubbish.'

'You haven't seen the underbelly. You don't understand what a huge privilege it is just to be Western. Financially, I mean. Spiritually, of course, we're utterly impoverished. That's why we're prone to this kind of breakdown.'

'But . . . she's . . . how long has she been like this?'

'Oh, a few weeks.'

'And all because Liz shagged Ping.'

'That was just the final straw, but basically, yes.'

'Jesus.'

'I mean it's stupid really, because Ping slept with everybody.'

'What?'

'It was part of the tuition, I suppose. If he thought you were getting somewhere, he'd help you go Tantric.'

'What – even you?'

'No – I deliberately didn't let him find my centre, because I wanted Caz to have a chance to get there first. She'd had her thing for so long that I kind of hoped if I acted coldly towards Ping, he'd get the message and concentrate on Caz.'

'And did he?'

'No. That's the tragedy. He concentrated on Liz. By the looks of things he found her centre quicker than he found Caz's knee.'

'Centre? Is that – like – your . . . ?'

'No. Don't be disgusting. Don't you know what Intimate Yoga is?'

'Of course I don't.'

'It's a way of finding the central point of the bodies' energies through the laying on of hands of a qualified Intimate Yogi.'

'Laying on of hands?'

'Exactly. He teaches the whole group the basic position, then, while you're meditating, he comes up to you one by one and manipulates you into position. When you've found a perfect balance and are at peace, he lays his hands on, and together you locate your centre.'

'Where was yours?'

'I never found it exactly, but it was somewhere here.'

She crossed her legs and sat bolt upright, then placed the fingers of her right hand a fraction above where the pubes would have started.

'Wow! Is that where everyone's centre is?'

'It depends. It's different for each person.'

'Don't tell me. Fat old people have it on their shoulder, and young nubile women tend to have it bang on their clit.'

'You are such a cynic. I don't know how you can live with yourself.'

'This guy's a genius. Where was Caz's centre?'

'You can't ask that. It's a very personal question. If you know where someone's centre is, you know an awful lot about them.'

'Go on. I won't tell anyone. Where was it?'

'Look – she never found it exactly.'

'Roughly. Where was he looking?'

'Well – she only vaguely located it, but they did manage to pin it down to somewhere here, in the crook of the elbow.'

'See?'

'What are you saying?'

'Nothing. Just that he didn't fancy her. Let's face it – who wants to get in bed with a skeleton.'

'She's not deaf, you know. You're being very hurtful.'

'This Intimate Yoga guy is a genius. It's like – people

pay him, and all he has to do is grope them, and they go away happy.'

'He *is* a genius, as it happens, and he wouldn't even understand the concept of groping. His mind is on higher things.'

'Yeah, sure. I'm going to have to learn how to do this.'

'He's a highly qualified man. You have to study at the International Headquarters of Intimate Yoga for at least five years before you get a teacher's certificate.'

'International Headquarters?'

'In San Francisco.'

'This isn't just one guy groping women in a shed in the arse-end of India?'

'It's an international movement.'

'That's incredible! So all over the world, at this precise moment, there are hundreds of women being Intimately Yogaed.'

'I suppose so.'

'What an amazing thought.'

Ranj then reappeared, and pulled me aside to tell me that he'd just met the East Sweden Women's Handball Team, who were taking a break from their tour of South Asia, and that he'd arranged to meet up with them on the beach for a midnight Punjabi lesson.

'How many people are there in a handball team?' I said.

'I dunno, but there's seven of them. That might include reserves.'

'You're incredible. Fee – do you want to meet up later for a midnight Punjabi lesson? This is my friend Ranj. He's the tutor.'

Fee's face brightened up at the sight of an Indian. She gave me an impressed smile for managing to befriend a local.

'So . . . you're . . . David's . . . friend?' enunciated Fee, in the style of a 1950s *Blue Peter* presenter.

'Fuck, yeah. He's a stormin' geezer,' said Ranj.

'Oh, right,' said Fee, blushing.

Don't you think you've had enough fun for the moment?

The weird thing about our midnight Punjabi party was that I ignored the how-to-identify-different-parts-of-Swedish-anatomy session, which took place amid much squealing, and ended up spending the entire time talking to Fee.

Now I know I hated her guts from the first instant I laid eyes on her, and I know she's a fake and a snob and a basket-case, but I have to admit that in the circumstances, I started finding her attractive. I think it might have had something to do with Caz's breakdown. Fee's over-the-top public-schooliness now had the edge taken off it, and she had picked up a sad, slightly subdued quality that was quite a turn-on. There's something about unhappy women that always gives me the horn.

Fee seemed to have given up on most of the spiritual crap, and the two of us could just sit and chat about everyday things, only mildly put off by Caz's presence. She said that she was only wearing the sari because the ashram had made her give away all her old clothes, and she hadn't got around to buying any new ones yet.

After we'd been talking for an hour or so, while we heard Ranj linger over an utterly implausible number of Punjabi words for 'nipple', a flirty edge started entering our conversation. The sound of the lapping ocean, the moon shadows from leaning palm trees, the distant music drifting down the beach and the nipple-talk all combined to produce an atmosphere heavy with the urgent need for copulation.

'How long were you and Liz going out together?' asked Fee, slightly coyly.

'A while.'

'Was it . . . good?'

'What – sexually?' I said, with a slight pout.

She shrugged.

I did a few instant calculations, deciding that a 'no' might make me sound like a bad lover, but a 'yes' would sound like a brush-off. The truth would give me away as the world's most spectacular loser.

'It was OK, but I've had better,' I said, impressed with my powers of diplomacy.

'What was . . . wrong with it?'

'Oh, you know Liz. She's very pushy. Not . . .' I put my hand on Fee's leg '. . . exactly what you'd call a sensitive person. And that came out in her love-making.'

'I hate her,' said Fee. 'I hate her more than anyone else in the world.'

'I'm not too keen on her myself.'

'I wish I could . . . could . . .'

'Duff her up?'

'Yes. Duff her up.' This sounded stupid in Fee's accent, and made us both smile.

'You know what would really piss her off?' I said.

'Tell me.'

'Well – me and her aren't, like, an item any more, but she's still a very jealous person, and if I went off with someone else, it would really get under her skin. 'Specially if it was someone she knew.'

Fee looked at me, blinking twice, but basically looking dead into my eyes. I held her gaze, smirking slightly.

'Are you saying what I think you're saying?' said Fee, leaning forward a touch.

'I don't know. What do you think I'm saying?' I said, also leaning forward.

'You tell me what you're saying, and I'll tell you if I think that's what you're saying,' said Fee, leaning forward some more. There was now about an inch between our lips.

'I think you should tell me what you think I'm saying, then I can tell you if that was what I was actually saying,' I said, leaning forward by about half an inch.

'It looks like we've reached a stalemate, then,' she said, filling in the remaining space, and placing us lip to lip.

The only courteous thing to do in the circumstances was to snog her.

She was, without doubt, the worst kisser I'd ever had the misfortune to tangle with. I felt as if my tongue was being vacuum-cleaned and put through a washing-machine spin cycle at the same time.

I was rescued from serious tongue cramps by Ranj suggesting that we all head back to the Kovalam Ashok Beach Resort to raid our mini bars. A few of the Swedes bottled out, but Ranj crammed into a rickshaw with three of them, I shared another one with Fee and Caz, and the seven of us drove up the hill to our hotel.

After we had gunned down the contents of my mini bar, Ranj took the three Swedes next door, and I stayed behind with Fee and Caz.

'So – here we are, then,' I said.

'Here we are.'

There was a silence.

Since there didn't seem to be much to discuss, I walked over and kissed her. In order to keep my oral mutilation to a minimum, I tried to undress her at the same time, which turned out to be a process rather like unwrapping a mummy, and wasn't exactly something you could casually do with one hand while trying to get your other hand into the bra. I eventually came up with a technique where she stood still, and I walked round and round her with an ever-swelling bundle of cloth, kissing her each time I went past her face. This was perfectly entertaining, but I didn't feel it exactly made for great foreplay.

We finally ended up on the bed, dressed in only our pants, doing the old writhe-around-and-grunt-a-lot thing that you do when you're trying to pretend you're turned on. When Fee started making the grunts that you do when you really are turned on, I started to feel a bit embarrassed.

'What about Caz?' I said.

We stopped for a moment, sat up and observed Caz, who was sitting bolt upright in a chair, staring at the opposite wall and rocking slightly faster than usual.

'She's fine,' said Fee. 'She's not even looking.'

'Can we just leave her there?'

'What else can we do?'

'I don't know. Doesn't it make you feel a bit weird?'

'Not really. I'm used to it.'

'I've never been watched before, you know.'

'We could put her in the bathroom.'

'No – that would feel worse.'

'She's not actually looking. Besides, you might find it's a turn-on.'

'All right. I'll get a condom.'

'No. Don't.'

'What – are you on the Pill?'

'No. I want to have non-penetrative sex.'

'Non-penetrative sex? What the fuck is non-penetrative sex?'

'Sex without penetration, obviously.'

'How can you have sex without penetration?'

'You do . . . other things.'

'It's a contradiction in terms. Like non-bike cycling.'

She shut me up by snogging me a little more, then giving me a blow-job. This was all quite embarrassing, because whenever I opened my eyes, I kept on seeing Caz. After a while, I noticed that Caz wasn't even staring at the wall any more – she had swivelled round and was staring right at me, her eyes slightly narrowed and red with anger. It's genuinely off-putting to have someone stare you in the eye while you're trying to enjoy fellatio, but fortunately Fee's disastrous snogging technique made for fantastic head, so my concentration wasn't too badly dented, and I ended up coming right in her mouth. She instantly spat it out on to the carpet, which I thought was a bit rude, and asked me if I had any chewing-gum or sweets. The only thing I could find was some hash, so we had a joint to get the taste out of her mouth – which was a relief because all the sexual vibes evaporated, so I didn't really feel I had to return the favour.

'Are you sure Caz is all right?' I said.

She was still staring at us, her eyes now even redder, burning with what looked suspiciously like psychotic fury.

'She can't really sleep in an upright position, unfortunately. Is there room in here for her? She doesn't take up much space.'

'I suppose so. But you go in the middle. I don't want to go anywhere near her. She looks nutty.'

'Don't worry. She's probably just tired.'

We finished the joint, then Fee made me turn my back while she undressed Caz and ushered her into our bed.

The following morning I was woken up by the sounds of an argument coming through the wall.

'No, no, no. Absolutely not,' a man was shouting. 'This kind of thing cannot be permitted. We are not some kind of cheap brothel. You people have no morals.'

I then heard Ranj's voice float clearly through the wall. 'It's my room, I can do what I want.'

'It's my hotel, and I simply can't allow it. Ordering four breakfasts from a single room is most irregular, and the poor young man who delivered the food is still in shock at the sight which greeted him. I must think of my staff first and I am going to have to eject you from the hotel.'

'Is there a rule book, or something? It doesn't say anywhere that you can't share your bed.'

'On your registration form, it expresses the right of the management to dispose of undesirables, and this is what I am doing.'

I then heard the door to Ranj's room shut, and a few seconds later, there was a knock on mine.

'Come in,' I called, assuming it was Ranj.

An Indian man in a smart suit timidly entered the room. 'I'm terribly sorry to disturb you, sir, but I am afraid that due to a problem with your compatriot, I will be having to terminate . . .' As his sentence tailed away, I saw the colour drain from his cheeks. 'Oh, my God! Heavens above! This one's at it too!' He turned his back, and started to rant in the direction of the door. 'It's a three-in-a-bed! I thought I'd seen everything, but now I have two English gentlemen entertaining multiple girls on the same night. First it's a gang-bang, and now I find a three-in-a-bed. This is just the limit. Please – the pair of you will be out of my hotel in less than half an hour. You people are animals. You have no morality whatsoever.'

'You don't understand. We weren't . . . I mean she's just . . . That's just her friend. We couldn't leave her in the chair.'

'I'm not interested in your practices. Just leave my hotel, and never darken its doors again.'

With that, he marched out and slammed the door.

Ranj then appeared in my room, with a huge grin on his face, followed by the three Swedes, dressed only in bra and panties.

'This is hilarious,' he said. 'I've never been chucked out of a hotel before.'

'But we weren't . . .'

'And he got you as well. We were listening through the wall, pissing ourselves. *First a gang-bang, now a three-in-a-bed*. Priceless.'

'We weren't, though. There just wasn't anywhere else for Caz to sleep.'

'Whatever. This hotel's a boring shit-heap, anyway. How about we join up with these fine young ladies at the Moon Cottage Hotel? It's right down by the beach.'

'Will you pass me my boxers?'

He chucked over some underwear, which I put on under the sheet. I noticed that Caz had somehow slept through the whole thing, while Fee was seemingly in shock – staring at the wall opposite and generally acting a bit like Caz.

I got out of bed and gave her a gentle pat on the arm.

'Fee? I think you should get up.'

'No,' she said.

'Pardon?'

At that moment, her mouth opened wide, and she started yelling at the top of her voice. 'NOOOOOOO! I CAN'T! I CAN'T GET OUT OF BED! THIS IS THE MOST COMFORTABLE BED IN THE WORLD! I CAN'T! I CAN'T I CAN'T I CAN'T! NOOOOOOO!'

The hotel manager charged back into the room.

'WHAT IS THIS RACKET? YOU...' Then, catching sight of the half-naked Swedes, he spun round to face the wall. 'Oh my God! This is too much! I cannot cope with this.' Now *he* was almost crying. 'Please. Clothe these women. I simply cannot have it. And this noise is simply intolerable...'

'NOOOOOOO! I CAN'T GO! I CAN'T GO!'

'I have other guests to consider. You are ruining the reputation of this establishment.'

'IT'S A BED! A REAL BED! I HAVE TO SLEEP IN A REAL BED! I'M NEVER GOING TO SLEEP ON ONE OF THOSE WOODEN BOARDS AGAIN! NEVER! NEVERNEVERNEVER! AND THERE'S A CARPET! I NEED THE CARPET!'

'Get this shrieking harpy out of my hotel.'

Caz chose that moment to wake up. Seeing Fee wail, her face instantly crumpled, and she sat bolt upright, exposing her breasts to the room. She started rocking faster than ever, twisting her hair around one finger and moaning to herself at a disturbingly high pitch.

'It's an asylum!' shrieked the hotel manager.

'Don't worry,' said one of the Swedes. 'The girls are a little upset. We'll cheer them up again, and then we can all leave. Don't worry.' She put an arm on the manager's shoulder, causing him to yelp.

The manager, his face a livid red with the pain of not looking at the sublime tits hovering just underneath his chin, wriggled out from under her arm. 'You have twenty minutes, then I'm calling the police.'

He marched out, suavely tripping over a chair leg on the way and slamming the door behind him.

The same Swedish girl then walked up to the bed, and put her arm around Fee, who was now moaning in competition with Caz. 'You're not happy, yes?'

'I CAN'T GO! I CAN'T! IT'S A PROPER BED!'

The Swede looked at me.

'They've been having a hard time lately,' I said.

'Do you want to go home?' she said.

'I CAN'T. I CAN'T. I'VE GOT TWO WEEKS LEFT. I CAN'T GIVE UP NOW. I'VE NEARLY FINISHED. I CAN'T GIVE UP NOW.'

'Don't you think you've had enough fun for the moment? You might be happier at home.'

'BUT I'VE NEARLY FINISHED. I CAN'T GO NOW.'

'There's no more beds here now. This is your last one until you go home.'

This set her off again.

'NOOOO! I CAN'T GET UP! IT'S A PROPER BED. NOOOO!'

'NOOOOOOO!' wailed Caz, her first word for more than a month.

'Well,' said the Swede, 'how would you like if we take you into town now? We ring your parents and explain that you are not happy, then we go to a ticket agent and book you to go home, asking that your father pays on a credit card, yes? That way, you will be back in a proper bed before you can think about it. You won't have to sleep on a hard bed ever again.'

'Do you think so?'

'Maybe one last night, then you can go straight to a proper bed.'

'Really?'

'Of course. You two . . .' she turned to Ranj and me, who were cowering in the corner, and clicked her fingers at us. 'Go outside and I'll make her dressed. What's her name?'

'Fee.'

'And her friend?'

'Caz.'

'OK. Now go.'

We stumbled next door while the nubile half-naked Swedes stayed behind to help dress the mad Englishwomen.

In silence, I watched Ranj getting dressed and packed. After a few minutes, the half-naked Swedes ushered in the now fully clothed Fee and Caz, and I went back next door, still in my boxer shorts. In the corridor, I noticed twenty or so chambermaids crowded around the fire exit, staring at me with their eyes on stalks. I shrugged at them and slunk away.

Ranj, who had spent the week practising his uncle's signature, paid the bill with an elegantly flourished American Express Gold Card. That afternoon, the competent Swede rang Fee and Caz's parents who, by the sound of things, embarked on nervous breakdowns of their own in England. Fee's mum took charge and booked flights from the Air India office in London, arranging for us to pick up the tickets at Trivandrum airport.

The earliest flights she could get were for a couple of days later, so we took turns acting as bodyguards. While Fee had taken a major backwards step since the three-in-a-bed episode, Caz seemed to have taken a turn for the better and had progressed from total silence to near-permanent gibbering.

A whole gang of us took them on the bus to Trivandrum airport, picked up their tickets, then let them loose into the departure lounge. The two of them staggered off in worryingly different directions. The chances of them getting on the right plane in Trivandrum seemed slim enough, let alone of changing flights successfully in Bombay, but there was nothing more we could do. Presumably, if you stumble around an international airport for long enough, someone eventually puts you on a plane going in vaguely the right direction.

By this stage I had told Ranj all about the background to Fee and Caz's breakdowns, a story which sent him into paroxysms of glee. He insisted that I told only an edited version to the Swedes, leaving out enough for Ranj to be able to pose as a master of Intimate Yoga.

He held off until Fee and Caz had left, but on the very day of their flight he let slip a few words about his yogic mastery, and afternoon sessions on the beach soon became a regular part of the day.

All of the Swedes, except for the goalkeeper, turned out to be centred on various parts of the upper inner thigh or extreme lower abdomen.

Peace

Dear Mum & Dad,

I'm sorry about the last postcard, but I was feeling a bit low at the time. I'm now having an amazing time. I've met up with this really nice Indian guy who's been paying for me to stay at an expensive hotel with him. We're having a brilliant laugh together and have just moved down to a smaller hotel near the beach, so that we can be nearer the action. I'll be home soon.

                    love,
                    Dave

PS Apparently Liz has been sleeping with a yoga guru in Rajasthan. If you bump into her parents, pass this on.

Dear Grandad,

I'm having a brilliant time. India has been a fascinating experience which has changed me enormously.
Some of the railways here still have steam trains in operation!
I hope you're well.

                    love,
                    Dave

When the Swedes finally left, Ranj slumped into a depression. By this stage I only had a week left in India, so we agreed that Ranj would go home, apologize and get engaged, while I got the train to Delhi. This journey covered the entire length of the country, and according to The Book took forty-eight hours, which, if I left a spare day for emergencies and three days in Delhi for reconfirming my flight home, meant that I had to get a move on.

Ranj and I took a depressed trip into Trivandrum together, and he headed to the airport to see what flights he could get to the Punjab, while I went to the railway station. Back on the beach, we looked at our little slips of paper as if they were death warrants. Well – he did, anyway. I was actually quite pleased to be going home, even if it did temporarily seem like a bit of a shame to be leaving Kovalam behind. In fact, if I'm honest, I was so excited about going back to England that I could hardly get to sleep that night.

On the morning of my train, Ranj got up early and waved me off from the hotel door. We exchanged addresses and phone numbers, but the whole thing was a bit of a sham, and it was obvious that we'd never really see each other again. If we ever met up in London, it would probably spoil things. I didn't want to meet the Putney Ranj. He'd probably be just another ordinary Asian bloke, and he'd spoil my memories of India Ranj, the priceless nutter.

On the train to Delhi, I felt that I was already on my way home, and had the strange sensation that more than anything else this was exactly what I wanted to be doing. I didn't want to *be* at home, I wanted to be going home. All the difficult stuff was behind me, and the long train journey back to the capital felt like a lap of honour. Staring out of the window while I returned to my starting point, I began to feel all colonial about things – as if I was surveying territory that I had conquered. The longer the journey lasted, the more impressed with myself I became. Such a huge distance, and it was all mine – I'd done it all. I couldn't believe that I'd actually covered so much ground on my own – and without getting killed, robbed or eaten.

For the entire forty-eight-hour journey, I stared out of the window in a state of serene calm, or slept the dreamless sleep of a freshly crowned Olympic champion.

Back in Delhi, I returned to Mrs Colaço's guest-house and even managed to get the same dormitory bed as last time. I sat on the hard mattress for a while, cross-legged, and contemplated how cool I was. I had actually done it. I was back where I started, and I was still alive. I felt years older and infinitely wiser than when I'd last been in the same place. I had lasted the entire three months without giving up and going home. The trip was a success.

I still didn't really know what travellers were supposed to do all day, but that didn't seem to matter. I *was* a traveller. I'd been to places and done things that most people avoid out of fear. I had suffered, and confronted dark sides of myself. I had experienced the world.

After a while, two nervous guys in clean-looking jeans walked in, claimed a pair of beds, then sat there in silence, looking as if a bomb had just exploded inside their heads. I noticed that they still had airline tags on their backpacks.

'Hi,' said one of them.

'Peace – er, I mean hi,' I said. 'You just arrived?'

'Yeah.'

'You feeling a bit out of it?'

'Jeeeesus,' groaned the other one. 'It's so *hot*. I can't believe this. How are you supposed to do anything here?'

'You're not, really. Do nothing. Whatever.'

'Right.' He looked at me as if I was talking nonsense.

'How long have you been here?' said his friend.

'Oh, long enough. I'm off home in a couple of days.'

'Starting uni?'

'Err . . . yeah. I suppose so.'

'What are you reading?'

'A John Grisham thing. I can't remember the title.'

'No – I mean, at university. What subject?'

'Oh, right. Um . . . English.'

'Really? Where?'

'York. You on a year off?' I asked, trying to change the subject. I wasn't ready to think about home yet.

'Yeah.'

'Just starting?'

'Yeah. We're doing a couple of months here, then hopefully a month in Pakistan, then Thailand, Indonesia and Australia.'

'Cool.'

'Bit daunting, actually.'

'You'll be fine,' I said, thinking that they were certain to get cripplingly ill at some point, not to mention depression, loneliness, despair, robbery, homesickness, and the fact that they'd probably end up hating each other's guts. 'You should have a laugh.'

Seeing these fresh-faced scared little bunnies about to head off around India reminded me how pleased I was that I'd got the whole thing over with. In the end, I was glad I'd done it, but I had to admit that the having done it was more fun than the doing it. Crapping your pants, for example, is a dire and miserable experience; but having crapped your pants – I mean, that's a pretty good conversational party-piece. I'd get a lot a mileage out of my dog-burger story. In fact, ten years on it would probably end up being the only thing I remembered, regardless of the fact that in all likelihood it wasn't even dog meat in the burger. I could already feel that the dog-burger story was taking pride of place among my India anecdotes. Based on what I'd heard from other travellers, this story had just the right combination of silly-little-me-I-shouldn't-have-done-it-ness and I'm-so-hard-I-dealt-with-it-anyway-ness.

It was obvious that no one would ever ask me what the mountains looked like, or how the climate changed around the country – they'd just want to know if I shagged anyone, and how ill I'd got. Luckily for me I'd done both (sort of), so I'd always have something to show for my trip. And whatever happened to me for the whole rest of my life, however boring I became, I would always be able to say that I had gone round India for three months on my own. I mean, I hadn't done the *whole* thing on my own, but what the hell – I could say what I wanted.

A completely different person

My take-off time was six-thirty in the morning, and it said on my ticket that I had to check in three hours early, so there was hardly any point in going to bed. I managed to get the hotel to arrange a rickshaw for two in the morning, and I spent the evening reading, then went to the meeting place that I had agreed with the driver.

He was fast asleep in the driver's cabin, and I tapped him on the arm a few times without any luck. Only when I gave him a pinch did he actually wake up. His head sprang from his folded arms, and he looked at me with startled and panicked eyes, until he remembered who I was. He then grunted and stumbled to a tap in a nearby wall. After having doused his face, he staggered back to the rickshaw, started it up, and we drove off.

All over the city, we passed rickshaw drivers asleep in their little cabins. I hadn't realized that they didn't go home at the end of the day. I felt suddenly guilty, as it occurred to me that maybe I'd been a bit meaner than was strictly necessary – haggling over every rupee on every journey. This emotion was instantly swamped, however, by a surge of relief. I realized that for the entire three months, nagging little moments of guilt like this had been gnawing away at me, and in only a few hours I'd be free of it all, for ever.

It was hard to tell from behind, but my driver's lolling head and wobbly steering gave the distinct impression that he was asleep for a significant portion of the journey. Despite a few close calls, I was still alive when we arrived at the airport, so I gave him a generous tip. A cynic would say that I was just offloading a load of useless currency on the first person I could think of, but I genuinely did want to tip him. If I'd known how little money rickshaw drivers made, I would have tipped all of them.

At first sight the airport was utterly deserted, but after a brief wander I spotted a small group of people in one distant corner of the huge check-in hall. It turned out that this group consisted of five other travellers, all of whom were getting the same flight as me. There was Brian, a BT phone engineer who'd just finished his trip-of-a-lifetime and was worried that he wouldn't get his job back; his nameless sulking girlfriend with her nose in a Jilly Cooper; Lionel, a trainee chiropodist from Lancashire; Oompt, a German engineering student; and his friend Litty, who was doing a PhD on ground frost.

We sat around and chatted for a while, until Oompt mentioned that he had a Frisbee in his rucksack. Four of us then got up and started playing a huge game of long-distance indoor Frisbee, covering half the length of the building.

While we were playing, I noticed a strange albino-looking woman in an all-white sari step through the doors. When I saw the rucksack in her luggage trolley, I realized she wasn't an albino, but was probably a Westerner with shameless taste in clothes. Then, when her head turned towards us, I froze and the Frisbee hit me in the face.

Oh my God! It was Liz. She may have been wearing Indian clothes, but it was definitely her. She still had the same effortfully serene walk.

I tossed the Frisbee to Oompt, retired from the game and watched her take a seat in the furthest corner of the departure hall. I wasn't sure whether or not she had seen me. After a moment of indecision, I started walking towards her with my heart pumping fast. I tried to breathe slowly in order to help mask my anxiety, but this just got me out of breath and made me look even more anxious.

When I got close, I saw that not only was she in a white sari, she even had one of those red blobs on her forehead. What a twat!

'Hi!'

'Hi.'

She shot me a sneer, then looked away. I had felt briefly sympathetic towards her, seeing her turn up at the airport all on her own, but when I saw that scornful look, I was instantly reminded of how much I hated her.

I decided to be friendly, though, since I knew that was the best way to annoy her.

'Isn't this amazing?'

'What?'

'Us. Both here.'

'We are booked on the same flight, you know. It's not exactly what I'd call a huge surprise.'

'Oh, yeah. I'd forgotten about that.'

She glared at me, and silence descended.

'When you first walked in, I thought you were an albino.'

'Very funny.'

'Then I saw it was you, and I couldn't believe it! Dressed in all this gear.'

'I've simply adapted to the Indian climate and culture. That is the point of coming here, in case you hadn't realized.'

'Looks weird, though. You're going to stand out a mile on the Piccadilly line.'

'My parents are picking me up, actually.'

'You going to stop wearing this stuff when you get home, then?'

'What do you mean by home?'

'Home. Your mum and dad's house.'

'I don't consider that to be home any more. I've moved on.'

'Where's home, then?'

'Wherever I want it to be.'

'So you're going to stick with the sari, then?'

She looked at me contemptuously.

'I'll probably adapt to England when I arrive, but for the time being I can't actually remember what it's like.'

'Cold. Wet.'

'Still a moaner, I see.'

'That's not a moan. I'm glad to be going back. I've had a laugh, but – you know – I've got to get on with my life.'

As those words came out of my mouth, I felt my head go dizzy. Suddenly, for the first time, it hit me that I really was about to go home. I was about to climb into a metal box that would take me back to England, and back to real life. In just over a fortnight, I'd be starting university. I'd have to work – read proper books – write things.

'Get on with your life? That's typical. You're a typical Western careerist.'

'Why – what are you planning to do? You're not going to be able to keep up this hippie-bullshit act in England, you know. It's back to the real world, now.'

'I can't believe that you've still got the same attitude. You've spent three months here, and the whole experience just hasn't made the slightest dent.'

'Dent? Hasn't made a dent? Believe me – I've been through a whole car crash here. I'm a completely different person.'

'Yeah, right.'

'I am.'

218

'How?'

'I'm just . . . you know, much more grown up. I *was* a kid – now I'm a proper, confident adult.'

'You were far too cocky in the first place, Dave. I don't think increased confidence is exactly going to turn you into a better person.'

'Cocky is different from confident. That's exactly the point. Kids are cocky, adults are quietly confident.'

'And you're quietly confident now, are you?'

'If you want to put it like that, yes.'

She creased up with laughter.

'Fuck off, Liz. I don't need this.'

'You're hilarious.'

'Don't patronize me, you pretentious bitch.'

'Ooh! Is this you being quietly confident?'

She started laughing again.

'Look – sort yourself out, here. If you're going to act like this, I . . . I might just find myself telling James about you and your Intimate Yoga man.'

The laughter stopped.

'Where did you hear that?'

'From a certain little birdie I bumped into. And we got on rather well, as it happens.'

'You bumped into . . . ?'

'I shan't say more. But they told me exactly what happened.'

'Look, Dave – don't let's forget that you spent the majority of the year trying to shag your best mate's girlfriend, which doesn't put you in much of a position to blackmail.'

'Who said anything about blackmail? I just suggested that we try and make an effort to sustain some kind of civil relationship. Neither of us wants rumours circulating in England, do we?'

She gave me one of her spine-tinglingly evil looks.

'With any luck, we'll never see each other again,' she said, lifting a book from her lap and starting to read.

I watched her reading for a few seconds until it became clear that, as usual, Liz had got the last word.

'Let's hope so,' I muttered half-heartedly and loped off.

PART THREE

Dave the traveller

Something unrealistic

Driving home from Heathrow, I felt almost as if I was seeing London for the first time. I was amazed by how clean it all was, how there were proper roads with pavements everywhere, how all the shops had enormous glass windows at the front, how the only animals were plump little dogs on leads, and how all the cars moved around as if they were in a road-safety film. No one seemed to be just hanging out – people were all marching around, purposefully going somewhere. Everyone was in their own little bubble, hidden behind glass, or a raincoat, or even just a fast walk.

And for some reason English number-plates all looked really silly. The whole place seemed more like a kind of Toytown than a city. There was something unrealistic about everything – as if it was all a parody of silly little England.

The first thing I did when I walked through the front door was to gulp down a glass of water straight from the tap. What a luxury! Mum offered to cook me whatever I wanted, and I asked for a steak with green beans and new potatoes. She instantly produced it all from the fridge and started cooking, saying that she'd known exactly what I'd want and had bought it all in advance.

While I ate, she asked me so many questions about the trip that I somehow failed to tell her anything. The minute I embarked on a story, she'd interrupt me after a couple of sentences to ask what I'd eaten, where I'd slept, how I'd washed my clothes, and all sorts of tedious crap which somehow stopped me from ever explaining what the trip had actually felt like. The more I talked, the less I seemed to explain anything. She just couldn't understand what I was talking about. There was simply no point of contact between her world and mine. It was like trying to explain the rules of basketball to a jellyfish.

Before long, she lost interest and started telling me about everything that had happened at home since I left, none of which seemed to amount to anything. As far as I could tell, everything was exactly the same as before, and yet her version of the last three months took up almost as much time as mine. Watching her jabber away, I was amazed that she could talk at such length without it dawning on her how boring she was.

The steak, which was stunningly delicious, gave me stomach cramps. I hadn't tried to digest anything that solid for months – in fact, my dog-burger was probably the only meal I'd eaten in India that had required any chewing.

I put a thumb in my mouth and did a quick check to see if my teeth were all still properly attached, then went for a stroll to try and walk off the stomach pain. The weather was simply gorgeous – a grey sky, with scudding clouds blotting out the sun, and a deliciously chilly wind that gave me goose-bumps on my arms. It was such a joy to be cold – to feel the crisp air in my throat and chest, with the wind stinging my cheeks, and my nose turning red. I stood still and took my first proper lungful of English air. Aahhh!

Trudging through the soggy grass of my local park, I was struck by the incredible greenness of everything. I'd become used to lurid food and brown landscapes, but suddenly everything was the other way round. Again, it all looked slightly unconvincing. Nothing felt quite real. I started touching and squeezing things for extra confirmation of their existence – plucking strands of grass, stroking a wet bench and twanging leaves from their branches.

On the way home from the park, I popped into my local corner shop for a bar of proper, real, English Dairy Milk chocolate. (You can get a version of the same thing in India, with the same wrapper, but it has the texture of pastry.) I had the usual 'All right, mate, how's things, Arsenal aren't looking too good' conversation with the guy behind the counter, then found myself asking him where he was from.

He gave me a weird look.

'I've just been in India,' I explained. 'That's why you haven't seen me for a while.'

'Oh, right!' he said, smiling broadly. In fifteen years of using his shop I realized that I'd never particularly seen him smile before. 'Gujarat,' he said. 'Originally my family's from Gujarat.'

'Cool. I only passed through Gujarat. What's it like?'

'Ah – very beautiful. The most beautiful place in the world. You shouldn't ask me, though, I'm biased.'

'When d'you come here, then?'

'I was fourteen.'

'Fourteen!'

'Yeah. I go back once each year. To see my family.'

'Right.'

'Where did you visit, then?'

'Oh, I flew to Delhi, then I went up to Himachal Pradesh . . .'

'Aah – Himachal Pradesh is beautiful.'

'Amazing. That bit was incredible. Then I went across to Rajasthan, down to Goa . . .'

'By plane?'

'Train and bus, mainly.'

'You went from Rajasthan to Goa without flying? Are you crazy?'

'I didn't really know how far it was. I kind of regretted it, actually. Then I went down to Bangalore and on to Kerala.'

'I've never visited the south. One day, maybe – but with work and children . . .'

'It's tough.'

'Mmm.'

'You should go. It's beautiful.'

'So I've been told.'

'It really is amazing.'

'Will you ever go back?' he said.

'Me?'

'Yes.'

'God – I haven't really thought about it. You know – it's hard work travelling there. It's not exactly relaxing. But . . . maybe in a few years . . . if I get another chance. Yeah, I wouldn't mind going back.'

Our conversation tailed away, and I wandered outside feeling oddly perturbed that I was already saying I wanted to go back to India. After only a few hours in England, all the unpleasant parts of my trip were tumbling from my memory. Rationally, I could still just about weigh things up and remember that for the majority of the time I'd been miserable, but I felt so happy that I'd done it, and had survived, that my positive emotions were already beginning to swamp everything else. In my mind, the trip was turning itself into an amorphous *good thing*. I was becoming incapable of reconciling the pleasure of having done it with the misery of doing it, and the feeling of pleasure was so immediate, and so powerful, that it swept away all rival emotions. I couldn't *really* remember what the agonizing bus journeys had felt like – I couldn't revisit the sensation of having that brutally hard seat slap my bruised arse and throw me on to the floor, but I *could* remember what I'd seen out of the window and how the first glimpse of the mountains had made my heart surge.

All my contradictory feelings were passing through a filter which was picking out anything unpleasant or painful. I could already sense that I was going to end up with clear, uncomplicated, positive memories. My journey round India was already reducing itself into just another person's 'amazing experience'.

I'm going to have to do this

I'd been home for a couple of days when I got a phone call from James. There was such a lot to say and, more importantly, such a lot to avoid saying, that I kept our phone conversation short and arranged to meet up in a pub later. I didn't mention Liz, and hoped she wouldn't come, but I noticed him using the word 'we' where he ought to have been saying 'I', which I took as an ominous sign.

That evening, both of them turned up at the pub together, arm in arm. My heart sank. I had no idea what she had told him about our trip, and how much I would be able to say without contradicting her.

James was significantly skinnier than I remembered him, and his neat hair had been transformed into a straggly mop which dangled in blonde waves on either side of his now tuftily bearded face. He was wearing sandals, jeans and a stretched, misshapen T-shirt. He used to look like Richard Clayderman as school prefect, but now he was Jesus-with-a-hangover as student-union rep.

Liz was wearing a short skirt and a body-hugging top that made my balls gurgle. The sari and the red spot had vanished.

As soon as James saw me, he screamed my name across

the whole length of the pub, then bounded over and gave me a hug. This was rather intimidating, since it meant that either he still didn't know what had happened, or he knew everything, and was biding his time before he planted a knife in my back. Liz smiled and gave me a peck on the cheek. There was no trace of India left in her body language.

With James at the bar queuing for drinks, the atmosphere instantly thickened. Liz stared at me blankly, giving nothing away, while I stared at her, trying to guess what on earth she could be thinking.

'You ditched the sari, then?' I said, eventually.

'What's it to you?'

I shrugged.

'Have you told him?' I said.

'Told him *what*?'

'About us.'

'There's nothing to tell.'

'Right. Silly me.'

'I just said that we went, had fun and came back.'

'You didn't even tell him that we separated?'

'No.'

'Why not?'

'Because I don't want to have to lie to him, so I told him about the trip without really mentioning you.'

'You lied to him because you don't want to have to lie to him.'

'Oh, God. Here we go again. Dave and his tedious games.'

'Don't start, Liz. I'd just like to know what I can and can't say.'

'As little as possible, if you can manage that for once.'

'Oh, so I'm the talkative one now, am I? That's rich.'

'Drop it. He's coming back.'

James arrived at the table to find us shining brittle

smiles at one another. Liz put her arm around him and, for my benefit, gave him a sexy kiss on the neck.

'You're a lucky man,' I said, with a sarcasm pitched only for Liz.

'I certainly am,' said James, smiling wanly and stroking her arm.

'So how was your trip, then?' I said.

'Incredible. Best thing I've ever done. And yours?'

'Yeah – good. You know, there were a few difficult bits, but – basically – it was an amazing experience.'

'Liz somehow persuaded you to leave cosy little England?'

'Somehow.'

'How did she do it, then? You always said you never wanted to go further away than Watford.'

'You know – she's a persuasive person.'

'You're telling me.'

'It was a mutual decision,' said Liz. 'A marriage of convenience.'

'And you two got on OK?'

There was a longlish pause in which we avoided catching one another's eye.

'Like a house on fire,' I said, in a tone of voice which made it sound like a distinctly odd metaphor for social harmony.

A silence descended, with James eyeing us suspiciously.

'Did something happen?' he asked.

'Like what?' I said.

'Between you two.'

Liz and I both looked at our glasses.

'I'm getting a weird feeling,' James continued, 'that you two . . .'

'What?' Liz's lips were pursed, white with tension.

'. . . didn't get on, or something.'

I felt myself and Liz both deflate slightly with relief. James wasn't about to guess the truth.

Then I suddenly wondered why I should feel relieved. I didn't have to lie for Liz. I was under no obligation to her. She had treated me like an arsehole and had deserted me in the middle of India. There was no reason why I had to lie on her behalf in order to help sustain her doomed, dishonest relationship. I had almost forgotten the vital fact that I hated her guts. The only real issue was my friendship with James, but if he carried on going out with Liz, then that was all over, anyway.

In a sudden, light-headed moment, I realized that I had nothing to lose. I could have some fun.

'You know what?' I said, with a grin. 'I thought you were going to say that you thought we'd slept together.'

James burst out laughing. I burst out laughing. Confusion running riot over Liz's features, she also forced out a few chuckles and began to bite her nails.

When the laughter died down, I smiled at her and said, 'Did *you* think he was going to say that?'

She gave me an evil stare by way of an answer.

'You didn't get on, did you?' said James.

'Oh, we got on well at first,' I said. 'We were very close, weren't we?'

I was enjoying this. Liz was suffering like I'd never seen her suffer before. For the first time since we had become friends, I was in control.

'James,' said Liz, in a suddenly sharp tone of voice, 'we have to leave.'

'Why?'

'Because I can't sit round a table with this creep any longer.'

'Are you being serious?' he said.

'I don't want to come between you and your friends, but if he's going to act like this, I'm just going to have to tell you the truth about what happened.'

The grave look on her face brought James up short, and he began to look worried. 'What did happen?' he said.

'I didn't want to have to tell you, because I knew it would upset you Basically, Dave and I went to India as friends, but from the moment we landed he didn't stop pestering me for sex.'

'WHAT?' I screamed.

'He used the threat of abandoning me as a way to try and wheedle sexual favours out of me. I did my best to fend him off, but he was so persistent that in the end, the only thing for me to do was to run away.'

James's face went red with rage.

'For fuck's sake, James. You don't believe that, do you?'

He glared at me.

'The girl's a pathological liar. You know that as well as I do.'

James was now squirming in his chair with anger and confusion.

'Dave,' he said finally. 'I'm a pacifist, but I'm going to have to do this.'

'What?'

He stood up and punched me in the face.

I was thrown off my stool and landed noisily on the floor. I heard the pub go quiet. For a few seconds I lay sprawled on the beery carpet, too shocked to feel any pain. Then my cheek started throbbing, I felt a wetness in my mouth, and my ear began to ring.

I staggered to my feet, clutching the side of my face. The whole pub remained silent.

'You know she's a fucking liar, James. She always has been. And she can't even lie very well. The whole thing's bullshit.'

'Why shouldn't I believe her?' said James, discreetly massaging one of his knuckles.

'You want to know the truth? After you left, we became good friends. Then we became lovers. Then we went to India. Then we fell out and separated. It's as simple as that.'

'FUCK OFF! We were *never* lovers. He always wanted me, James – from the instant you left the country – but I never let him get close. He's a disgusting prick, and I hate him.'

Everyone in the pub was now looking at James, to see what he would do next. Silence hung in the air, time suspended. The hush was eventually broken by a woman's voice from the far end of the bar, speaking with a thick Irish accent.

'Don't you b'lieve her, boy. That girl's got "liar" writt'n all over her nasty little face.'

Everyone spun round to look at the speaker. She gave one nod, and took a self-conscious sip of her gin and tonic.

'Take her at her word, son,' said the barman. 'You won't find another one better than that in a hurry.'

'Fuck off!' came a voice from near the fruit machines. 'If you can't put mates before birds, you're the scum of the earth.'

'Maybe that's why you haven't had a shag for three years,' came a woman's voice from a table near the door.

'Too right,' said another woman. 'He had your girlfriend, young man. I can see it from here.'

'Hit him again,' said the barman. 'You've got my permission.'

'Lay one finger on him, and I'll kick your fucking head in,' said the guy at the fruit machine.

'The woman's a slut!' said a pissed man, throwing his glass on to the floor. 'A faithless whore like the rest of them.'

'Who are you calling whores?' chorused the two women by the door.

Amidst a rising cacophony of voices, I felt myself going weak at the knees as the pain in my cheek surged to a new level. I righted my stool and sank back on to it. James and Liz remained standing, and I saw James put his arm around her shoulders. Behind him, a large brawl now seemed to be in progress.

Picking their way through the flying fists, they made their way to the door.

Dave the traveller

I had two weeks left before university was due to start and decided to try and focus my energies on the reading list that I had received for my course. I just about managed to get through the list, and even made a start on one of the books.

As for a social life, I decided that it was time to start again. I was about to begin in a new place, with a new load of people, so it didn't really matter that I'd made enemies of my two closest friends. In fact, it was a positive thing. Over the course of my big trip, I had matured so much that I was almost a new person. The time had come to cut all my old ties anyway, because people from my past would only have tied me back to my old self. As a new person, the time was right to clear the way for new friends. That was the whole point of university. I would be able to begin again as the new me – not as Dave the mediocre North London schoolboy, not as Dave the sexual failure, but as Dave the traveller.

PENGUIN ESSENTIALS

Eva Luna by Isabel Allende

Lucky Jim by Kingsley Amis

Regeneration by Pat Barker

Out of Africa by Karen Blixen

An Ice-Cream War by William Boyd

Any Human Heart by William Boyd

A Start in Life by Anita Brookner

A Clockwork Orange by Anthony Burgess

Junky by William S. Burroughs

Breakfast at Tiffany's by Truman Capote

In Cold Blood by Truman Capote

A Month in the Country by J. L. Carr

The Big Sleep by Raymond Chandler

Heart of Darkness by Joseph Conrad

The Man in the High Castle by Philip K. Dick

My Family and Other Animals by Gerald Durrell

The Circle by Dave Eggers

Invisible Man by Ralph Ellison

The Great Gatsby by F. Scott Fitzgerald

Tender is the Night by F. Scott Fitzgerald

PENGUIN ESSENTIALS

A Room with a View by E.M. Forster

Cold Comfort Farm by Stella Gibbons

Goodbye to All That by Robert Graves

The Diary of a Nobody by George and Weedon Grossmith

The Reluctant Fundamentalist by Mohsin Hamid

The Thin Man by Dashiell Hammett

Steppenwolf by Hermann Hesse

I'm the King of the Castle by Susan Hill

High Fidelity by Nick Hornby

Three Men in a Boat by Jerome K. Jerome

Dubliners by James Joyce

On the Road by Jack Kerouac

Lady Chatterley's Lover by D.H. Lawrence

The Periodic Table by Primo Levi

A Short History of Tractors in Ukrainian by Marina Lewycka

The Road to Lichfield by Penelope Lively

Lolita by Vladimir Nabokov

Wide Sargasso Sea by Jean Rhys

Bonjour Tristesse by Françoise Sagan

White Teeth by Zadie Smith

PENGUIN ESSENTIALS

The Prime of Miss Jean Brodie by Muriel Spark

Are You Experienced? by William Sutcliffe

Hell's Angels by Hunter S. Thompson

A Confederacy of Dunces by John Kennedy Toole

Cat's Cradle by Kurt Vonnegut

A Handful of Dust by Evelyn Waugh

Brideshead Revisited by Evelyn Waugh

Twilight by Elie Wiesel

The Day of the Triffids by John Wyndham

Mrs Dalloway by Virginia Woolf

PENGUIN ESSENTIALS

THE CIRCLE/DAVE EGGERS

**'SECRETS ARE LIES.
SHARING IS CARING.
PRIVACY IS THEFT.'**

The Circle – the world's most powerful company, connecting everyone digitally – is growing. Its latest recruit is Mae Holland. Determined to prove she is worthy of the trust placed in her, Mae allows herself to go 'transparent', sharing her every experience with the world at large. But in moving closer to those in charge, she catches glimpses of a sinister truth hidden at the very heart of the Circle. One that will change the world for ever . . .

'Prescient, important and very funny. The most-on-the-money satirical commentary on the early internet age' *Guardian*

THE RELUCTANT FUNDAMENTALIST/MOHSIN HAMID

**'I see I have alarmed you.
Do not be frightened by my beard.
I am a lover of America . . .'**

At a Lahore café one evening you meet a mysterious stranger. He asks you to join him for tea and, speaking impeccable English, he begins to tell you his story. It is the tale of how as a young man he went to America and embraced the Western dream and even took a Western lover. As the night darkens, you learn of the souring of his dream and his love, of his feelings of anger and betrayal. And finally the true reason for this chance meeting becomes abundantly clear . . .

'I closed the book with a shudder. Sharp, relevant, impressively intelligent. Entertains at the same time as it makes you think' *Daily Telegraph*

PENGUIN ESSENTIALS

WHITE TEETH/ZADIE SMITH

'While he slipped in and out of consciousness, the position of the planets, the music of the spheres, the flap of a tiger-moth's diaphanous wings in Central Africa, and a whole bunch of other stuff that Makes Shit Happen had decided it was second-chance time for Archie . . .'

When fate steps in and roundly ruins divorced forty-seven-year-old Archie Jones' suicide attempt, he seizes his second life by the horns and promptly meets and marries Clara Bowden, a Caribbean girl twenty-eight years his junior. Thus begins a tale of friendship, love, war, three cultures and three families over three generations . . .

'A rollicking good read' *Independent*

A SHORT HISTORY OF TRACTORS IN UKRAINIAN/MARINA LEWYCKA

'Two years after my mother died, my father fell in love with a glamorous blonde Ukrainian divorcée. He was eighty-four and she was thirty-six . . .'

Voluptuous gold-digger Valentina loves green satin underwear, boil-in-the-bag cooking and, she insists, the émigré father of sisters Vera and Nadezhda. Putting aside a lifetime's feuding, the sisters will do anything to protect their father. Unfortunately for them, he doesn't want to be saved. Worse, the sisters' battle to keep their father from Valentina's clutches unearths troubling family secrets that reach back fifty years into Europe's dark history . . .

'Mad and hilarious' *Daily Telegraph*

PENGUIN ESSENTIALS

ANY HUMAN HEART/WILLIAM BOYD

'I have to start my real life soon, before I die of boredom and frustration . . .'

Logan Mountstuart – writer, lover, art dealer, spy – navigates his way through the twentieth century. In Paris he meets Hemingway and in London he argues with Virginia Woolf. Recruited as an agent by Ian Fleming, he is betrayed in the war and fetches up in sixties New York as artists begin to flock there. Throughout he seeks what each of us seeks – love, happiness and fulfilment – yet he makes the same mistakes we all do in finding it. Here, then, is a journey deep into a *very* human heart . . .

'Superb, wonderful, enjoyable' *Guardian*

TWILIGHT/ELIE WIESEL

'As a boy, Raphael feared madness but was drawn to madmen.'

A professor of literature and a Holocaust survivor, Raphael longs to find Pedro, the man who rescued him as an orphan in postwar Poland. But Pedro vanished inside the prisons of Stalin's Russia. When a mysterious caller directs him to the Mountain Clinic, an asylum for those whose delusions spring from the Bible, he finds patients calling themselves Adam, Cain, Abraham, Joseph, Jeremiah, and God. Searching for Pedro among them, Raphael seeks the meaning of his own survival . . .

'Wiesel has the literary talent and the moral ferocity to make our daily concerns seem trivial' *New York Times*

PENGUIN ESSENTIALS

A START IN LIFE/ANITA BROOKNER

'Dr Weiss, at forty, knew that her life had been ruined by literature.'

Beautiful, intelligent but lonely academic Ruth Weiss studies Balzac trying to work out exactly where her own life went wrong. Yet as she finds herself examining her childhood in London, the friendships that once meant so much to her and the ill-fated relationships she embarked on in Paris, she sees that her life has not been quite the series of missteps she had once thought. That perhaps there is still a chance at happiness, a new start . . .

'Enormously sophisticated, knowing, often very funny tragi-comedy' *Financial Times*

THE ROAD TO LICHFIELD/PENELOPE LIVELY

'The tide's against us, hadn't you noticed? People haven't got that much time for the past nowadays'

Anne Linton is living a split life. Her father has suffered a stroke and most weekends she abandons her family and takes the road to Lichfield to be with him before he dies. But the longer she spends there, the more she is drawn into another life. Over a lingering summer she embarks on an affair, tries to save an old cottage from developers and discovers that her own father was not entirely the man she has always imagined him to be. As she begins to see the influence of the past everywhere she turns, Anne's present becomes more and more uncertain . . .

'Unfailingly literate, thoughtful and touching' *Washington Post*

PENGUIN ESSENTIALS

THE DIARY OF A NOBODY/GEORGE GROSSMITH AND WEEDON GROSSMITH

'I fail to see - because I do not happen to be a "Somebody" - why my diary should not be interesting'

Mr Pooter is a man of modest ambition, content with his clerkly lot. So why is he always in trouble with disagreeable tradesmen, impudent young clerks and wayward friends? And what is he to do about his son Lupin's distinctly unsuitable choice of bride? However hard he tries, life piles its little mishaps on his head - but he's not about to give up.

The Diary of a Nobody is a sharp, hilarious satire of suburban values and remains as pertinent now as it was when it was first published a hundred years ago.

'The funniest book in the world' Evelyn Waugh

THE THIN MAN/DASHIELL HAMMETT

'When I opened my eyes and sat up in bed some six hours later Nora was shaking me and a man with a gun in his hand was standing in the bedroom doorway'

Ex-detective Nick Charles attracts trouble like a magnet. He thinks his sleuthing days are over, but when Julia Wolf, a former acquaintance, is found dead, her body riddled with bullets, Nick – along with his glamorous wife, Nora – can't resist making a few enquiries. Clyde Miller Wynant, Julia's lover and boss, has disappeared. Everyone is after him, but Nick is not convinced Wynant is the murderer – and when he finds a junked-up hoodlum with a careless attitude to guns in his bedroom, it's only the beginning of his troubles.

Set among the speakeasies of early 1930s Manhattan, *The Thin Man* is hardboiled crime at its wisecracking best.

'Harsh lights and romantic black shadows: this is the heyday of American crime writing' *Guardian*

PENGUIN ESSENTIALS

THREE MEN IN A BOAT/JEROME K. JEROME

'Let your boat of life be light, packed with only what you need - a homely home and simple pleasures, one or two friends, worth the name, someone to love and someone to love you, a cat, a dog, and a pipe or two, enough to eat and enough to wear, and a little more than enough to drink; for thirst is a dangerous thing.'

Suffering from every malady in the book except housemaid's knee, three men and a dog decide to head for a restful vacation on the Thames. Anticipating peace and leisure, they encounter, in fact, the joys of roughing it, of getting their boat stuck in locks, of being towed by amateurs, of having to eat their own cooking and, of course, of coping with the glorious English weather.

Three Men in a Boat is the hilarious story of what is probably the worst holiday in literature.

'I fell out of bed laughing' *Guardian*

DUBLINERS/JAMES JOYCE

'Snow was general all over Ireland. It was falling on every part of the dark central plain, on the treeless hills, falling softly upon the Bog of Allen and, farther westward, softly falling into the dark mutinous Shannon waves.'

From a child grappling with the death of a fallen priest, to a young woman's dilemma over whether to elope to Argentina with her lover, to the dance party at which a man discovers just how little he really knows about his wife, these fifteen stories bring the gritty realism of existence in Joyce's native Dublin to life.

Richly detailed, *Dubliners* is an unflinching, brilliantly compelling portrayal of ordinary lives and the moments that make them.

'Joyce's early stories remain undimmed in their brilliance' *Sunday Times*

PENGUIN ESSENTIALS

THE PERIODIC TABLE/PRIMO LEVI

'So it happens, therefore, that every element says something to someone'

Inspired by the rhythms of the Periodic Table, Primo Levi assesses his life in terms of the chemical elements he associates with his past. From his birth into an Italian Jewish family through his training as a chemist, to the pain and darkness of the Holocaust and its aftermath, Levi reflects on the difficult course of his life in this heartfelt and deeply moving book.

Written with characteristically understated eloquence, *The Periodic Table* is one of the key testaments of the last century.

'A book it is necessary to read' Saul Bellow

THE PRIME OF MISS JEAN BRODIE/MURIEL SPARK

'Give me a girl at an impressionable age, and she is mine for life . . .'

Passionate, free-thinking and unconventional, Miss Brodie is a teacher who exerts a powerful influence over her group of 'special girls' at Marcia Blaine School. They are the Brodie set, the crème de la crème, each famous for something - Monica for mathematics, Eunice for swimming, Rose for sex - who are initiated into a world of adult games and extracurricular activities they will never forget. But the price they pay is their undivided loyalty . . .

The Prime of Miss Jean Brodie is a brilliantly comic novel featuring one of the most unforgettable characters in all literature.

'Spark's most celebrated novel' *Independent*

He just wanted a decent book to read ...

Not too much to ask, is it? It was in 1935 when Allen Lane, Managing Director of Bodley Head Publishers, stood on a platform at Exeter railway station looking for something good to read on his journey back to London. His choice was limited to popular magazines and poor-quality paperbacks – the same choice faced every day by the vast majority of readers, few of whom could afford hardbacks. Lane's disappointment and subsequent anger at the range of books generally available led him to found a company – and change the world.

'We believed in the existence in this country of a vast reading public for intelligent books at a low price, and staked everything on it'
Sir Allen Lane, 1902–1970, founder of Penguin Books

The quality paperback had arrived – and not just in bookshops. Lane was adamant that his Penguins should appear in chain stores and tobacconists, and should cost no more than a packet of cigarettes.

Reading habits (and cigarette prices) have changed since 1935, but Penguin still believes in publishing the best books for everybody to enjoy. We still believe that good design costs no more than bad design, and we still believe that quality books published passionately and responsibly make the world a better place.

So wherever you see the little bird – whether it's on a piece of prize-winning literary fiction or a celebrity autobiography, political tour de force or historical masterpiece, a serial-killer thriller, reference book, world classic or a piece of pure escapism – you can bet that it represents the very best that the genre has to offer.

Whatever you like to read – trust Penguin.